HOOK
The Duplicity Duet

ELISABETH GRACE

ISBN: 9781987925081

Cover design and photo by: Sarah Hansen at Okay Creations

Line Editor: Sheri Thomas

Proof Reader: Shawna Gavas at Behind The Writer

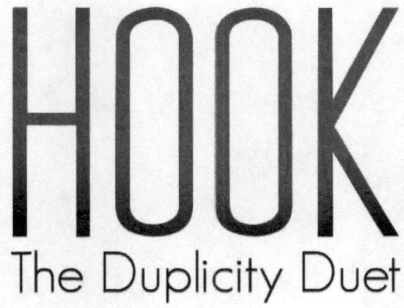

HOOK
The Duplicity Duet

DEDICATION

To all the good people who have done bad things.

I crumple to the floor as the reality that I've lost everything drags me down into an abyss. The lies and half-truths splinter my fragile heart into jagged pieces of glass, ripping me apart from the inside out. The eyes of the man I thought loved me bore into me from above, and the realization hits—he is the one responsible.

He did this.

My heart is a kiln that hardens my despair and transforms it into a rage so monstrous it cannot be contained. I've been forged in fire and born anew.

He would pay.

They all would.

I'd burn this whole cesspool of a city to the ground until I'd exacted revenge on all of them.

Every. Single. Fucking. One.

- Emily

ELISABETH GRACE

CHAPTER ONE

The first time I slept with a man for money I didn't come.

I was okay with it because, hey, it was my first time and I was nervous. But years later, I've grown tired of only experiencing the big 'O' through my own battery-operated devices. Being a high-end call girl, surely a perk of the job should be a climax every once in a while, right?

I squeezed my eyes shut, willing an orgasm to overtake me.

"Ah, that's it, Brandi. Just like that," Julian said as I ground my ass back into him.

His hands gripped my waist as he pounded in and out of me while I stroked my clit in hopes that—just this once—I'd find relief from something other than my vibrator.

"You almost there, baby?" he asked and then groaned.

"Almost," I panted. My time was running out. I attempted to clear my mind and forget my surroundings, hoping that would help. He plunged in and out, the mechanics of it all in place but the intended result so far away. A slight tingling was all I felt though, and I resigned myself once again to fake the orgasm.

"Ahh"—I began moaning—"oh, right there. That's it. Oh my God. Oh my God!" I fisted the sheets for extra effect. "Oh, Julian, I'm gonna come. I'm coming for you!" With that final proclamation, I threw my head back, causing my dark hair to cascade down my back.

It might've been a little theatrical, but it got the job done.

He thrust into me a couple more times. You know the ones I'm talking about—those jerky, off-rhythm movements that almost always mean a guy is about to finish. And finish he did, with a few grunts and whispered words about how I was the best fuck in Vegas.

Damn straight. You didn't get paid what I did a night because you were a limp lay.

I dropped down onto my stomach. Julian rolled onto his side and stroked lazy fingers across my naked back. Only a few minutes passed before he said, "I gotta run." His hand stopped stroking and he pressed a kiss to my shoulder.

I turned my head on the pillow to watch him crawl out bed, remove the condom and toss it in the trash before reaching for his clothes folded neatly on a nearby chaise.

We'd left the hotel curtains open, and though it was dark out, the chaotic, sparkling lights of Vegas provided enough ambient light for him to go about his business. My gaze wandered to the night sky in search of stars, but like always, there were none to be seen here. Growing up in Utah, there were always an abundance of stars. Then again, Vegas seemed to suck the light out of everyone, so I supposed it was fitting. Just another reason why I hated this wretched town.

The mattress sunk as Julian sat on the edge of the bed, drawing my thoughts back to the present.

"I wish I could stay longer." He leaned down and tucked my hair behind one ear.

"I'm sure I'll be seeing you soon." I sat up, not bothering to cover myself, comfortable in my nakedness. "I had a good time tonight."

His hand brushed the side of my breast before settling on my waist. "You know I always have a good time with you, Brandi."

I curved my lips into a smile, one designed for seduction, and leaned in, pressing a chaste kiss to his lips.

His hand at my waist gripped me tighter. "Got some business to take care of out of state. I'll make arrangements to see you when I'm back in town."

"Be careful," I said. He nodded and slipped back out of bed quietly to make his way out the door. Julian was in a dangerous line of work—to put it mildly. I didn't know specifics, but I knew enough not to ask questions.

I lay back down and gazed once again out at the night sky.

I enjoyed my evenings with Julian, as much as I was able. At least I always knew what to expect with him. He was a pretty average middle-aged guy with light brown hair and a fit body, and the best part was that he wasn't into kinky shit.

Once I was sure he wouldn't be returning, I rolled over and turned on the lamp. The expensive hotel room came into view, and I instantly spotted what I was looking for. On the corner of the nightstand sat a stack of bills that had been neatly arranged. I reached for it to tally my nightly earnings.

Counting off bills in my head as I placed them on the mattress in front of me, I realized that he'd left me a larger than usual tip.

I smiled to myself. My blowjob skills must have been on point tonight.

This is the part where you judge me. We both know that's what you're doing…but don't bother. It won't make any difference to me. I'm not in need of someone to save my fucking soul.

And no, I didn't get into prostitution because I had daddy issues, nor do I have a drug habit I'm trying to support.

I had my reasons.

As does anyone who's ever done something worthy of being judged.

A soft knock sounded at the door and the mechanism inside the lock clicked. The hulking frame of my bodyguard, Leroy, came into view as he stepped into the room.

"Hey, baby girl. Saw Julian book it out of here. How'd everything go?"

I held up the cash and shook it back and forth. "He was generous tonight."

I'm one of the agency's top earners, which means that Leroy accompanied me whenever I conducted *business*. All on the orders of my madam, Sylvia.

Since Julian was a long-time client, Leroy waited in the lobby rather than outside the door, giving him a little more leeway than he would a new-to-me john. I'm sure even Leroy tired of listening to my fake orgasms. God knows I got tired of performing them.

I stepped out of bed and approached the six-foot-five behemoth, unconcerned with my nudity. Long ago I'd resigned myself to the fact that my body was no longer private property. At this point, it was merely a vessel to do the job. It didn't really matter. I'd never noticed Leroy trying to sneak a peek anyway.

I pushed a small stack of bills at him. "This is Sylvia's take. Be sure she gets it?" He nodded, and I made my way around him to the bathroom to get dressed. After I'd put my dress back on and collected all my belongings, I returned to the room to find Leroy waiting for me by the door.

"How you know I'm not gonna rip you off? How come you always trust me to get this to her?" he asked as we exited the room.

I smiled and elbowed him in the ribs. "Because I know you for the softie you really are, and you'd never screw me over." It may seem peculiar to call a giant man a softie, but it was true.

Leroy was one of the only people I trusted in this town, and one of the very few who knew why I chose this profession. I knew he'd pass the money along to Sylvia rather than pocket it for himself.

Vegas wasn't called 'Sin City' for nothing, but despite what he did for a living, Leroy wasn't one of the sinners. Everyone else here was out for themselves and would turn their backs on you in a heartbeat. That included Sylvia. While my madam and I had a cordial relationship, I was just a way for her to make bank and we both knew it.

Leroy tousled my hair as we walked along the multicolored carpeting toward the elevators. "You always seein' the best in everything, aren't ya?"

"No, I see the truth. It's one of the things you need to survive this gig." He looked over at me with a mix of pity and compassion. "Don't give me that look," I said. "I don't want your pity. I'm blessed in my own way."

He wrapped his arm around my shoulders and tugged me to his side. When we reached the elevator doors, he gave me a squeeze and said, "That you are, baby girl, that you are."

A chuckle escaped my lips. Who would've ever thought a call girl could consider herself blessed?

Time to head home to the reason why I truly am.

CHAPTER TWO

A half-hour later, far from the stench of the strip, I pulled into the driveway of the modest ranch bungalow I rented in a picturesque, family-friendly community. Yes, there was such a thing in Vegas.

I hit the button that opened the garage and then drove inside, waiting until the door closed completely before exiting the car.

Creeping inside the house, I was careful not to let the door slam shut behind me. After setting my bag on the kitchen counter, I made my way down the hallway, to the back of the house like I always do, then peeked my head in the door of the bedroom that held the other half of my heart.

I stood there for a moment gazing upon the small, frail figure in the bed, watching to make sure his chest was rising and falling. Satisfied, I tiptoed toward the spare bed in the opposite corner of the room, where Martina, a nurse and now friend, was sleeping soundly.

I gently shook her shoulder, rousing her from sleep.

A weary smile spread across her face and she rubbed her eyes before sitting upright. Her long dark hair was pulled back into a ponytail with the odd piece falling down the side of her face.

"How did it go tonight?" I whispered.

"He did well. No issues at all," she whispered back, taking my hand and squeezing it. "How are you?" she asked with concern. Martina and I had known each other long enough that she was aware of what I did to earn a living. There were no secrets between us.

"Another day, another dollar." I squeezed her hand back.

She pursed her lips and nodded, then rose quietly from the bed. As she left the room, she whispered, "See you tomorrow night."

After checking once again to be sure his chest was still moving, I crept from the room and retreated to my master bath, where I ran the shower as hot as I could stand it. It had become something of a nightly ritual for me, scrubbing at my skin with the single-minded focus of removing any remnants of the night's activities.

I wasn't ashamed of what I did—not at all. But I had one life within the walls of this house and another outside of it. I'd created a sanctuary within this home that I would maintain at all costs.

Yes, I let men use my body. But I used them, too. I took their money, and in return I fulfilled their deepest fantasies without them having to feel ashamed. No one cared what a high-paid hooker thought of them.

I dried off after my shower and dressed quickly before slipping back into the bedroom where that small figure still lay, not having moved a muscle. He never did.

I put my hand just a hair's breadth above his chest until it rose, barely brushing my palm. Then I lay down beside him and curled into his little body before drifting off into a dreamless sleep.

CHAPTER THREE

"Mom?"

I stirred and opened my eyes, gritty from too little sleep. Rolling carefully to my side, making sure not to lie on his petite body, I smiled when I saw those blue eyes, so much like my own, gazing over at me.

I brushed a piece of my son's sandy brown hair off his forehead. "Morning, kiddo. How did you sleep?"

"Okay, I guess. How was work?"

Daniel thought that I bartended at one of the Vegas clubs, which accounted for my late hours, low-cut shirts, and overabundance of cash. And he'd keep right on thinking that.

"Busy, busy." I cupped his face and took in his innocent features. The way his nose was slightly upturned with a few freckles scattered across the bridge, reminded me of myself at his age. Instead of my dark brown hair, he'd gotten his father's sandy-colored hair.

"Mom..." he whined. His hand lifted up off his lap a few inches as if he wanted to remove my hand from his cheek. If only he were able. Daniel was always reminding me that he was nine years old now and no longer a baby. His body may have betrayed him, but in his own mind he was just a regular boy who didn't want his mother fawning all over him.

"All right. All right." I ruffled his hair and sat up in bed. "Are you hungry?" His eyes lit up at the mention of food. "I was thinking of making your favorite this morning— pancakes with chocolate chips and whipped cream."

"Awesome!" he cheered as joy filled his little face. "You're the best."

The warm feeling in my chest that only my son could produce wrapped around my heart like a blanket. "Let's get you up out of bed and empty your bladder. Then you can watch a cartoon until the pancakes are ready."

Daniel nodded as enthusiastically as he could. I stood from the bed then bent down and picked up his small frame. Walking him over to the corner of his room, I placed him in the custom-made electric wheelchair where he spent his days. I leaned in to give him a kiss on the cheek.

"Mom! What was that for?" he asked with a grimace.

"That's just because I'm your mom and I love you. Get used to it, buddy. I'll be doing it for the rest of your life. It's my right as your mother."

"If you say so," he grumbled before steering himself out of the room.

After helping Daniel in the bathroom, I followed behind as he rolled down the hall to the living room, where I turned the TV to his favorite channel. "Awesome. Skylanders is on," I heard him say as I headed to the kitchen to start breakfast. I smiled to myself, knowing how much he loved this show.

My kitchen wasn't a chef's paradise with its cream cabinets and glass subway tile backsplash, but it was large enough for Daniel to get his wheelchair in and out of so we could eat together. Anywhere it was easy for him to navigate was my kind of wonderful.

Satisfied I had all the necessary ingredients, I grabbed a cup from the cabinet and filled it with water. Pulling the handle to another cupboard, I picked up the pill bottles I needed and set them down in front of me.

Daniel was on several different medications—some for his muscle pain, others for his heart. I counted out exactly what he needed and pushed out of my mind, as I did every morning, the thought of what would become of Daniel if he didn't get his daily meds.

Carrying the glass of water and the pills, I returned to the living room and held them out in the palm of my hand so Daniel could see what I had. "It's that time again," I said, trying to keep my voice light. As if it were the most natural and enjoyable thing in the world to have to shove a cocktail of prescriptions down your son's throat every morning.

"When am I going to be able to take those myself?" There was mild irritation in his voice.

Daniel didn't like me doting on him, and I tried my best not to. I recognized the fact that he was getting older and now had his own free will demanding to be heard. He might've been ready for that change, but it didn't mean I was.

"Not for a while yet, buddy. I like to know that you've taken them."

He looked up at me under drawn eyebrows, clearly not pleased that I was stifling his independence, but took his medicine as instructed.

Twenty minutes later we were enjoying our breakfast

together when Daniel surprised me with a question out of the blue. "Mom, where is my dad now?"

My fork paused halfway to my mouth and my heart tripped over its usual rhythm, sputtering and then speeding up until all I heard was its pounding in my head.

The last time Daniel asked me about his father was well over a year ago. I knew at some point I'd have to field more questions, but he hadn't asked much more than who his father was and I hadn't offered more than the bare minimum, knowing no good could come of it.

I pressed my lips together while I considered my answer. Reaching across the table, I took his small hand in mine and gave it a squeeze. "I don't know where your father is, buddy. I'm sorry."

"Why didn't he want me?" His lips trembled, but he tried to puff his chest out as if the words didn't bother him.

I clutched my shirt because his pain was a physical ache in my chest.

"It wasn't that he didn't want you. I told you that before." Tears sprang to the corners of my eyes and I fought to gain control of my emotions, knowing I had to be strong for my son in this pivotal moment. "I was very young when I had you. You know that. Your father was just as young. When he found out he was going to be a dad he...he was scared." I cleared my throat while Daniel gazed across the table at me like I held all the answers. Which of course I did, but he wouldn't be getting them today. "Do you remember when you had to have that surgery a couple years ago? Remember how scared you were?"

Daniel gave a small nod of his head.

"That's how scared he was. He didn't feel like he'd be able to be a good father to you, so he decided to let Mommy do the job all on her own. He thought it would be better…for you." It sickened me to make excuses for that coward Damian, but I'd never allow my son to feel unwanted. "Does that make sense, buddy?"

I squeezed his hand again, willing the massive amount of love I had for this boy to seep through and somehow be enough to take the place of an absentee father.

"I think so." He still looked confused. "But he would be older now, right? How come he hasn't tried to find me?"

What my son lacked in physicality, he more than made up for in intelligence—a fact that was proving difficult for me at the moment. "Maybe he lives really far away. Or maybe he doesn't know how to find us. I'm really not sure. Could be he still thinks I'm the best person for the job."

A small smile formed on his face. "You do a great job, Mom."

The stabbing sensation in my chest melted away into a warm, radiant feeling, like sunbeams hitting your face on a summer's day. "You make it easy, kiddo." I reached forward and ruffled his hair then quickly shoved a bite in my mouth, praying this line of questioning was over.

"After I'm done, can I watch another episode of Skylanders?" he asked around a mouthful of pancake.

"Daniel, don't talk with your mouth full, please."

He swallowed. "Can I though?" He had such a hopeful expression on his face that I hated to deny him.

I glanced up at the kitchen clock. "Lily will be here soon for your therapy session. I want to finish that history lesson we were working on yesterday before she gets here."

Daniel stuck out his bottom lip—he could act like a petulant child when he wanted to—and got back to eating his breakfast.

Originally, I began homeschooling Daniel because I thought it'd be easier for him, but over the years I've realized that it's my own selfish way to keep him close to me. He's my *whole* world. My entire reason for being. And whether it made me a helicopter parent or not, I wanted him with me always. Our time together would be cut short because of his condition, and I wasn't willing to part with him a moment more than I had to.

It killed a piece of my soul every night I had to leave for work, but the money I brought in ensured that I could give my son the best therapies, medications and doctors available. And it was worth every penny. They had made such a difference in Daniel's life, keeping him healthy and allowing him to prosper to his body's fullest potential, despite his rare form of muscular dystrophy. At his age, many children with the disease were already on ventilators. Daniel was one of the lucky ones.

Beyond keeping my son in good health, I had *big* plans for the two of us, and as soon as I was able to set aside enough money, I was going to make them a reality.

To the outside world, we may just be a hooker and her sick son—and I knew better than most that the world didn't owe us anything. Early on, life had handed me that lesson on a tarnished silver platter. But I'd be damned if I sat back and let life roll right on over us, leaving its tread marks behind.

No, the plans I had for us didn't involve accepting defeat.

CHAPTER FOUR

Like always, Daniel was exhausted after his physical therapy session with Lily. I put him to bed to sleep for a while, and since I had some time to myself, I poured a cup of tea and turned on the computer.

I'd been taking online business courses for years in an effort to achieve my ultimate goal of one day opening a center to support other children with muscular dystrophy. I envisioned a place where families that couldn't afford proper care and treatment would be able to receive it, an environment where every child who suffered from the same debilitating disease wouldn't feel different or alone.

I would not be a statistic. I refused to be.

Not only was I a single mother, I was a single mother of a child with special needs.

Society might look down their noses at my chosen profession, but I was supporting myself and my son. I wasn't relying on the system, so why should they care that my pussy paid the bills?

I decided to check the local MLS commercial listings before I got started on my coursework. I'd been keeping an eye on the market so I'd have an idea of what it was going to take to make my dream happen. I loved browsing through the ads and daydreaming about the possibilities of making it *really* happen.

I clicked through the first few listings. Nothing interesting there. They'd all been on the market for a while. The screen displayed the next listing and I sucked in a breath.

A mid-sized white building was being listed in a good area of town, not too far from one of the hospitals. I scrolled through the pictures and something bloomed inside me.

Hope.

There couldn't have been a better building if I'd built one from scratch myself. All the room sizes appeared to work, the building didn't seem to be falling apart, and it had a handicap ramp out front. I could picture perfectly in my mind how welcoming the place could be with a few renovations.

I sat there imagining desperate families walking through the door and leaving with dignity and hope, and I knew I needed to do whatever it took to make it happen.

I had to see for myself if this place was really as good as it appeared to be. Hopefully it wasn't like most things in Vegas—all flash and no substance.

"Mom, this isn't the way to the grocery store," Daniel said from the back of the van.

Yes, a hooker driving a wheelchair-accessible minivan—bet you don't see that every day.

"I know, bud. I want to drive by a building that just went up for sale." I scanned both directions after the light turned green before proceeding into the intersection.

"Are we moving?" he asked, not sounding thrilled at the idea.

"We're not moving. This is for the center."

I glanced in the rearview mirror just in time to see Daniel's grin almost split his face. Smiling, I made another turn. "Almost there."

As I made my way down the street, I double-checked the address written on the scrap of paper in my hand. A minute later, the property came into view.

It was perfect. The neighboring buildings seemed to be well cared for—one housing an ophthalmologist, and the other appeared to be some type of marketing and graphics design business.

I was imagining what it would look like with a parking lot full of cars and a sign out front when Daniel asked, "Are you gonna buy it?"

He sounded so hopeful that a small part of me felt like a terrible mother for bringing him here to see it with me.

"It's a lot of money." My shoulders slumped. "Money I don't have at the moment."

There was silence for a beat as we both sat in the air-conditioned van, staring out the window at the place.

"Mom?"

"Yeah, buddy?"

"If anyone can find a way to do it, you can."

There was such unwavering confidence in his little voice that I had to squeeze my eyes shut for a moment to compose myself. I swear sometimes it was as if that child climbed into my soul, knew exactly what I needed to hear, and delivered it.

"Maybe someday." I cleared my throat and adopted a light tone. "Should we go get some groceries so we don't have to eat stale cereal for the next week?"

"Can I get Lucky Charms?"

I rolled my eyes at his usual attempt at sucking me into buying that crap and then pulled the van away from the curb, more committed than ever to making the center a reality.

We arrived at the grocery store a few minutes later, and after helping Daniel out of the van, we headed into the store. I grabbed a cart from the front and we began gathering all the items on our list.

We'd been in the store for about twenty minutes, all the while I'd been thinking about that building and how desperate I was to get my hands on it.

"You passed the tomato sauce." Daniel's voice drew me out of my thoughts, and I turned to look over my shoulder. He'd parked his electric wheelchair in front of the display of the brand we normally purchased. *Smarty pants.*

I laughed and wheeled the cart back around in the opposite direction. "Now how did I walk right past that?" I reached for the jar and placed it in the cart.

He smiled with a mixture of sadness and understanding. "You were thinking about the center." His gnarled arm reached out and patted my hand weakly. "Don't worry. It'll work out however it's supposed to. It always does."

My boy was wise beyond his years. Soulful. He always had been.

I bent down and placed a chaste kiss on his cheek. "Ugh. Mom!" he said with obvious disgust. "What was that for?" He might have been wise beyond his years, but he was still a nine-year-old boy who didn't want his mom kissing him in public.

"Just for being you."

His eyes softened a little before he purposely adopted the disaffected features that only adolescents could pull off.

"What's next on the list?" I asked.

"Soup."

"That's in the next aisle over." I nodded my head in the direction we needed to go.

"What are you waiting for? Race you." He laughed as his wheelchair charged forward down the long grocery aisle.

I giggled and wheeled the cart down the aisle, pretending I was unable to catch him. When we reached the end of the aisle, we both sprinted out at the same time. Without warning, a cart banged into the side of Daniel's chair.

"Watch where the hell you're going!"

I abandoned my cart and rushed over to see if my son was okay. "Oh my God! Daniel, are you okay?"

He nodded in rapid, jerky movements, and his eyes looked about ready to pop out of his head. With my hands cupping his face, I did a quick head-to-toe scan and was happy to find that he was, in fact, unhurt. His chair was all in one piece which was an added bonus.

"Teach your retard kid how to drive that thing."

I immediately stilled, every last muscle in my body drawing tighter than an already stretched rubber band.

Slowly, I turned to confront whoever had made the disgusting comment.

An older man, probably in his early sixties, stood behind his own cart. His red, bulbous nose attracted my attention first, and he wore a shirt that looked like it hadn't seen a washing machine in at least a decade.

"You need to apologize," I ground out, fists clenched

at my sides.

"For what? He shouldn't be screwing around in the store." The smell of alcohol wafted over to me as the degenerate scratched at his protruding stomach through his t-shirt.

The veins in my neck expanded as the simmering rage from my chest erupted and spewed hate-filled venom throughout my body.

"For your crass comment about my son." I was trying really hard to maintain some sort of civility since Daniel was witness to this encounter. I didn't want to lower myself to this guy's level with my son watching.

"Seems true from what I see." His gaze darted behind me to Daniel. "Kid can't even control how he drives that fucking thing."

Tears pricked the back of my eyes at the injustice of it all. My son was a better person than this man would ever be, and yet he was confined to a wheelchair to be judged by others. As if that made him any less than anyone else.

I opened my mouth to lay into the drunk when Daniel's soft voice sounded from behind me. "It's okay, Mom."

Instead of telling the sorry excuse for a human being what I thought of him, I inhaled slowly and squeezed my eyes shut before slowly opening them.

"One day you'll be in need of some compassion, and I hope you don't get an ounce of it." I turned around to look at Daniel. He didn't appear as upset as I would've expected him to. "Come on, buddy. Let's finish up."

I allowed Daniel to steer his chair in front of the cart and lead the way to the next aisle over. As I passed by the stranger, he looked right at me. "Not like he can help you with those fucked-up hands anyway," he mumbled so only I could hear him, then glared over in Daniel's direction for a second.

Before I could rip this disgusting waste of skin's head off his shoulders and shove it up his ass, I pushed the cart forward. I blinked back the tears so my son wouldn't know how affected I was by the man's words.

One thing was for sure, I was more committed than ever to finding a way to make my dream happen. These children deserved better than to be looked down upon by the dredges of society. I wanted to give the families of those afflicted with muscular dystrophy a safe haven—a place where they'd be loved and accepted for the wonderful human beings they were. A place where they were given the resources to live the best life possible. A home away from home where their disease didn't define them.

The only question was, how in the hell was I going to come up with a down payment to secure the property before it was sold to someone else?

CHAPTER FIVE

I pulled up in front of the Bellagio and handed my keys to the valet. After the bullshit in the grocery store earlier, the last thing I felt like doing was plastering a smile on my face and giving a client a good time.

Butterflies danced in my stomach as my heels clicked across the lobby. It was always the same when I met a new john for the first time. I had no idea what to expect, and a bunch of different sick and twisted scenarios always permeated my thoughts.

I was known for providing men with the GFE—the girlfriend experience.

Most of my clients weren't into the really fucked-up stuff, but I never knew exactly what I was going to get until the hotel room door closed behind me. This was why I preferred repeat customers—of which I had many.

The johns looking for the hard-core action or fetish shit usually booked girls who specialized in PSE—the porn star experience. Definitely not my thing.

As nervous as I was, when I saw Leroy standing in the lobby at our designated meeting spot, my nerves settled a bit.

The brightly colored glass works of art dangling from the center of the ceiling caught my eye as I made my way over to him. The hues were alive and vibrant—every shade in existence must be represented there. I also spied the colorful indoor garden through the archways on the far side of the gargantuan lobby area. The different colors and arrangements they came up with always amazed me.

The Bellagio was easily my favorite hotel on the strip. I'd dreamed of visiting Italy since I was young, and this was the closest I'd probably ever get to achieving that particular dream. Basking in the European sun just wasn't a priority for me.

"Lookin' good, baby girl," Leroy said when I reached him. "You ready for this?"

"Aren't I always?" He pressed his lips together but didn't respond. "So where are we headed?"

"Up to the Grand Lakeview Suite."

"High roller?" I asked.

Leroy shrugged. "Dunno. Sylvia checked him out. Said he was in town on business. Said you could get his name when you met him. His request."

This wasn't unusual. In my line of work, clients often didn't use their real names with the girls. Since Sylvia screened all potential clients, she always knew who they really were and it wasn't necessary for us to know. It made no difference to me whether the guy sticking his dick in me was named Tom, Dick, or Harry. Pun fully intended. As long as he paid to play, we were cool.

The elevator pinged, alerting us to its arrival. We

stepped inside and my breath grew shallow as we made our way to the top of the hotel. I pictured my son in my head. That would probably seem weird to some, but it served as a reminder of why I did this.

The doors opened and I put one Louboutin in front of the other as I walked down the hall, Leroy by my side. Drawing in a deep breath, I reminded myself how many times I'd done this. *Get in there. Put on the act. Get out.*

We came to a stop in front of the suite and I fiddled with the strap of the bag on my shoulder.

"What's the matter, baby girl?" Leroy asked. "You got more nerves than normal."

I gave him a reassuring smile. "Tough day, that's all."

He squeezed my shoulder then knocked on the door in front of us.

"Un momento," a muffled voice said through the door.

Great. A foreigner. Italian, if I wasn't mistaken. An image of a balding dark-haired man with a belly hanging over his belt and too much back hair came to mind. I mentally cringed but forced a smile on my face as I heard the shuffling from the other side of the door.

The man who opened the door was the complete opposite of the cringe-worthy image I'd conjured in my mind. He stood over six feet tall and wore a navy silk suit, fitted to perfection. The white button-down shirt was open at the collar, revealing tan, olive skin that set off deep brown eyes fringed with eyelashes any woman would give her right arm for. His hair was a dark mahogany brown and a little longer on top. I pegged him to be about a decade older than me, probably in his mid-to-late thirties.

"Bellissima," he said, his gaze raking over me from

head to toe. "And you are?" He his raised brow as he lifted my hand and kissed it.

Ah, this guy was definitely looking for the GFE. There was no need for him to treat me like I was something special when his bankroll had already secured my presence there. Still, I supposed it was a nice change from feeling like a possession being bought and sold.

I cleared my throat to buy some time, since I seemed to be suffering from a case of cotton mouth. "Brandi," I replied.

Rule number one—*never* give your real name.

"I wonder if you'll go down as smooth as the drink." His Italian accent was thick, but his knowledge of the English language was obviously good.

"I guess you'll have to let me know," I said with a saccharin smile. "And you are…"

One corner of his mouth quirked upward. "Marco Valenti," he said, finally returning my hand to me.

This man was smooth, intelligent, and oozed power. Not a combination I was unaccustomed to, given my livelihood, but there was something about this man, in particular, that drew me to him.

Rule number two—*never* fall for your client.

I stepped through the door and glanced back at Leroy. "Do you have a key?"

"Not yet." Leroy held out his hand, palm open. My client slapped the key card in his hand while Leroy continued to glare, doing his best to intimidate him. Leroy had told me once that he found it easier to intimidate them up front to try and avoid trouble in the first place. Mr. Valenti didn't look the least bit phased by Leroy, giving him a regal smile before closing the door in his face.

I stepped further into the suite's foyer, admiring the floor-to-ceiling windows that showcased the strip and the lake with the majestic fountain show below. My heels clicked on the marble floor as we passed by a pair of bedrooms on either side of the hallway before entering the circular living and dining room area. It was elegantly decorated, the perfect blend of sophistication and comfort, mixing different shades of champagne, purple, and beige throughout.

Mr. Valenti headed over to the bar to pour himself a drink at the wet bar. "Qualcosa da bere?" he asked, holding up an empty tumbler. "Drink?"

Normally, I would accept a drink if offered. My gut told me I'd need all my faculties, so I declined by shaking my head. A small smile curved the corner of his lips like he knew what I was thinking. Flustered, I turned around to take in the view of the fountains below. I wasn't able to hear the melody the water danced to, but it didn't make the display any less beautiful as the white lights illuminated each rise and fall of the liquid silver.

I felt him approach before I smelled him. Instinctively, I knew he was taking in the snug fit of my dress, the curve of my ass underneath the black silk, and the way my stilettos made my legs go on and on. It was all I could do not to part my lips on a sigh when the smell of his expensive cologne enveloped me as he moved closer.

"É una meraviglia da guardare. It's a wonder to behold, yes?"

I glanced to the side and found his eyes locked on mine as he sipped the amber liquid in his glass.

A shiver stole over my body, laced with both need and fear. Fear because this was the first time—ever—that I'd found myself attracted to a client.

I cleared my throat. "It's wonderful." *Time to move things along.* "We should discuss payment and what your preferences are." I turned and faced him.

Rule number three—*always* get your money first.

He said nothing for a beat, merely stared me down with those assessing eyes of his before speaking. "So quick to get down to business."

"It's nothing personal." I took a couple of steps toward him and trailed a finger down his chest. "I find it more enjoyable to get business out of the way so we can get down to the fun stuff," I said, lying through my teeth.

He gripped my wrist in his strong hand, making me feel small and vulnerable. I stiffened beneath his grip.

"A woman after my own heart." His thumb slid along the pulse point on my wrist, and my breath caught in my throat.

I continued once I'd recovered. "If I'm going to make this enjoyable for you, I need to know what you're into." I looked up at him through my lashes with the seductive face I'd perfected years ago.

"And I'd like to know your preferences," he said, his voice like silk, a small smile on his face.

"This isn't about me." No man wanted to be reminded that he was paying for sex, so I always tried to delicately dance around the subject. This guy was making it difficult though.

"I *want* to know what you like." His voice remained neutral, but there was an underlying edge to it.

What was his deal? Why did he care?

"Mr. Valenti, what I want is to please you." I ran a hand down the expensive fabric covering his chest and over his belt until I cupped him in my hand.

Damn. He was packing.

He snatched my wrist away almost immediately, but not before I felt him growing beneath my palm.

"It would please me for you to call me Marco when you are with me," he said with tension in his voice.

I nodded and attempted to once again get this business transaction under way. "What did you have in mind for our time together, *Marco*? Did you want me to get undressed, or do you prefer to do that?" I licked my lips for added effect.

"You will answer my question."

I heaved out a breath. "I like when a client is very specific about *their* needs."

"You have spirit, Brandi." I ignored the way his Italian accent wrapped around my name, making it sound like an endearment, even if it wasn't my real one. "I like it."

I took a step away from him, grateful when he didn't try to stop me. I needed some space to breathe. Marco's intensity was like an oppressive air in the room, pressing down on my chest.

I couldn't wrap my brain around why he'd care about *my* pleasure, but maybe that was his thing. He wanted to please women and prove what a competent lover he was in order to feed his ego.

Most clients had a thing. Some men pretended I was someone else, others wanted me to recite specific lines when they were inside me, and some were just looking to fuck in their favorite positions, ones their wives gave up long ago.

Marco leaned into me, his breath fanning across my face, causing goosebumps to race across my skin. "You're very stubborn for someone who's paid to provide me pleasure. É una fortuna che mi piacciono le sfide."

ELISABETH GRACE

"What was that?" I asked softly.

"Good thing I enjoy a challenge," he replied without blinking.

I cleared my throat, uncomfortable with the level of attention he was giving me. "Why don't we get on with what I'm here for," I suggested in a sultry voice.

His eyes narrowed. "As you wish. Your madam says you are like a..." He looked off toward the ceiling. "The animal that changes color."

"A chameleon?"

"That is the one." He smiled widely, showcasing a dimple in his left cheek, made more pronounced by the dark stubble on his jaw. As sudden as the ferocity had flared up inside of him, it quickly disappeared.

"It's true. I can be whatever you want," I replied in a seductive voice. I closed the distance between us, placing my hand on his chest. He flinched at the contact like I'd scorched him. Not a lot, but enough that I noticed.

Looking up into the depths of his dark eyes, I said, "Why don't you tell me what you're looking for, and then we can discuss any extras in my payment."

The smile dropped from his face and he reached for my wrist, pulling my hand from his chest. "What I want from you will be very different than most men."

My eyes widened and I sucked in a breath. This ought to be interesting. I'd had all manner of things proposed to me before, but the fact that Marco felt the need to warn me set off alarm bells ringing in my head.

"And what is it you want from me, Mr. Valenti?" I whispered.

"Call me Marco."

"Alright, Marco."

He traced his thumb along my hairline and stared down at me, intensity pouring out of his gaze like a waterfall. My breathing hitched, and I found myself wanting to lean into his caress to further close the distance between us.

Then the hum of his cell phone vibrating from his pocket broke our connection. He reached into his pocket, glanced briefly at the screen, and stepped back to take the call.

"As always, your timing is impeccable." The corners of his mouth dipped, and I had the distinct impression that he wasn't pleased with whoever was on the other end of the line.

Marco listened for a moment while staring out the wall of glass down to the strip below. His hand holding the phone flexed around it for a second at something the other person had said.

"Give me five minutes," he bit out.

Another pause.

"Well, if you want it to happen tonight, you have no choice but to wait." Without a goodbye, he ended the call and placed the phone back into the breast pocket of his suit jacket.

With his hands on his hips, he remained facing the window for a moment, drawing in deep breaths of air.

"I must go."

Not what I was expecting to hear. "Okay..."

He turned and stalked forward until only mere inches separated the two of us. His large hand came to rest at the swell of my hip before he leisurely dragged it across my waist and brushed the side of my breast with his palm. My nipples tightened inside my lace bra.

Marco dropped his hand and leaned into me. My

heart picked up pace inside my chest as I waited for his lips to touch mine. He stood solid and still before me while I waited, my anticipation like a live wire setting every nerve ending in my body on fire.

Just when I thought he'd close those final few inches, he brought his face alongside mine and his low voice sounded in my ear, "I'll get you your money."

His words were like a bucket of cold water, and I stepped back as if he'd slapped me. It pissed me off that *he'd* left *me* wanting.

He stalked back over to the bar and returned a moment later with an envelope. I eyed the cash inside before placing it in my purse. It seemed ridiculous to me that I'd be paid for having a conversation in the man's room for such a short time, but I wasn't about to argue with him about it.

"It's been a pleasure, Mr. Valenti." I made sure to use his last name since he'd asked me not to. I had a tendency to lash out when I was upset.

An amused grin formed on his face, but he said nothing. I strutted around him to the suite door.

As I unlocked the dead bolt then slid the chain across, Marco's hand landed on my ass, skimming over it a few times before his other hand pulled my hair to the side to expose my neck.

I hadn't even heard him come up behind me.

He pressed a kiss to the base of my neck and I shuddered, shivers racing up my spine. I felt his smile against my skin before he removed his lips and stepped away.

Without a backward glance, I turned the door handle and left the suite.

The warm feeling that had invaded my chest remained, but my stomach fell into a nauseous churning.

Somehow my body knew what I didn't already. Marco Valenti would be the springboard in my life that caused everything to change.

CHAPTER SIX

To my surprise, Marco Valenti booked my "services" again a few days later. Usually I was indifferent to who or what I would be doing on a particular evening, but when Sylvia called to inform me that he had requested my presence at his hotel suite again that evening, I wasn't wholly unaffected. No, in fact, I felt...anticipation?

This was new to me and I didn't like it. I was a businesswoman, plain and simple. My singular goal was—and always had been—profit.

I reminded myself of this as Leroy and I stood in front of the door to Marco's suite, waiting for him to answer.

"You okay, doll? You seem...nervous or somethin'."

"I'm fine," I said in my most convincing voice.

"You still on edge from last night? Don't worry, baby girl. Ain't no one gonna mess with ya tonight."

I gave Leroy a small smile that I hoped expressed my gratitude. Last night, my client had been a little overzealous roughing me up. Some guys were into that kind of thing, and as a rule I didn't prohibit rough sex, but this prick had smacked me, causing a small bruise to form on my cheekbone. *Asshole*. I'd had to press the pin in my necklace that alerted Leroy to my distress, and thankfully he'd intervened.

I'd been so deep in thought that I startled when the door to the suite swung open. That was the excuse I gave myself for why my heart was beating so rapidly in my chest. I refused to believe that it was the sexy-as-sin man standing in front of me, who'd obviously just gotten out of the shower. I made an honest effort to *try* not to envision that scene.

His dark locks were still damp, and the scent of soap and man wafted toward me as his half-lidded eyes leisurely roamed across my body. My nipples pebbled beneath my dress—that's *twice* now—and he gave me a knowing grin.

His slate gray suit pants hugged his muscular thighs while his crisp white dress shirt once again had the top three buttons undone. My gaze traveled lower to find him barefoot, and I couldn't stop myself from thinking that there was just something innately sexy about that.

"Brandi, how lovely to see you again."

Christ, I'd forgotten how delicious his accent made every word sound.

Just like the last time I saw him, Marco brought my hand to his mouth. However, instead of kissing the top of my hand, this time he placed a chaste kiss on the inside of my wrist, causing a swirling tornado of goosebumps to run up my arm. "Sei bellissima."

I'd chosen to wear a fitted black dress that went just past my knees and had a peekaboo cut-out at my cleavage. Along either side of my body was a strip of white fabric that ran from my armpits down to the bottom of the dress, creating an exaggerated silhouette of my waist and hips. Based on Marco's study of those curves, I'd say he appreciated the effect.

"I wasn't sure I'd be seeing you again." I nodded to Leroy and then entered the suite, Marco closing the door behind me.

"Were you pleased when you heard that I had requested your services again?" Marco asked from behind me as I made my way to the living area. I almost stumbled at his brazen question. If it had been any other client, I would've made a production about how happy I was to see them again. Somehow though it felt as if Marco knew the effect he had on me and was enjoying the fact that he'd gotten under my skin.

"I'd have to say that surprise was my strongest reaction." I set my purse on one of the side tables and turned to face the powerful man that had been stalking me down the hallway.

I sucked in a breath when we made eye contact. His long strides ate up the distance between us, and his eyes...his eyes were almost predatory—dark, glistening orbs that seemed to know way too much, to see way too much.

"I had endeavored to make a stronger impression than that."

"Is that so?"

"Sí."

"Well, you called me so I'd say that I was the one who made an impression." I smirked at him, enjoying our playful banter.

Marco, on the other hand, didn't seem to appreciate my sarcasm. His jaw tensed and his hand gripped me behind the neck, pulling us chest to chest.

"And why is that, I wonder?" His intense gaze skirted over my face, giving nothing away. The scent of him surrounded me, and how I wished at that moment that I could hold my breath for eternity. Between his proximity, his intensity, and the smell of him, I grew wet between my legs.

Marco was the first john to ever affect me this way. And I didn't like it. Not one bit.

While I'd longed to physically enjoy my job more than I had in the past, I still needed to keep my head clear. This was business—nothing more. Muddling that fact with any type of girly emotions or expectations was a disaster waiting to happen.

His large hand moved from beneath my hairline and wrapped around the front of my neck. My pulse quickened, and he must've been able to tell because one corner of his mouth quirked up with male satisfaction.

I held his gaze, refusing to cower and let him win this strange standoff we had going. As he smirked down at me, he released the hand from around my neck and traced an invisible path along my hairline.

An instant later, the smile dropped from his face.

"What is this under your eye?" His forehead creased as he extended his hand, pointing to the tender spot on my cheek.

My breath caught. *Shit.* I thought I'd done a good job of masking the bruise. No one wanted to pay thousands of dollars to spend the evening with damaged goods. I grazed the injury with my fingers, unsure how to respond.

Truth was, most johns didn't spend that much time looking into my eyes when they were with me, but as I was learning, Marco wasn't like most johns.

"It's nothing." Needing to get this evening back on

track, I trailed a finger down his hard chest. "Why don't we discuss what you have planned for us tonight?" I looked up at him through my lashes.

He gripped my wrist in his strong hand. It made me feel small and breakable, and visions of last night flashed through my head. I stiffened beneath his grip.

"Enough. I want to know what this is on your face." His lips pressed into a tight, straight line, and his jaw ticked.

I attempted to pull my wrist from his grip, but to no avail. "I'm here for a paid service, Mr. Valenti, nothing more." I held his gaze, trying my best not to quiver under his intense stare. I'd dealt with more difficult, more dangerous men than him before.

"You will call me Marco, *not* Mr. Valenti, when you are with me. If it's your money you're concerned with…" He let go of my wrist and walked back to the bar, grabbing something and then returning. "Here." He dropped an envelope on the small side table beside where I stood. "I assure you, it's all there."

I reached for the envelope, scanned the bills inside, and placed it in my purse, leaving it on the table. "Shall we get down to business then?" I licked my lips for added effect.

"You will answer my question," he snapped. "Your job is to do what I ask during our time together, is it not?"

I pressed my lips together. *He had me there.* "Fine. I was hit in the face last night. Can we move on?"

He took a step toward me, looking every inch the powerful and poisonous man I was sure he was. "Bella, who did such a thing?" I ignored the way his Italian accent wrapped around the endearment.

"It doesn't matter." I started to turn away from him to face the window, but he caught my upper arm and prevented me from doing so. I glanced down at his large hand, enjoying the way his long fingers wrapped around my pale skin. Mentally I scoffed at myself for having such a thought.

"It matters greatly," he said. The strangest thing was that I believed him. Everything about this man, from the sincerity in his voice, to his rigid stance, and his penetrating gaze, told me that it did matter to him.

I didn't want to explain, because no guy paying for sex wanted to think about the guy before him. It wasn't good business. But Marco wasn't leaving me much choice. I tried to think of some believable story on the spot, but I couldn't. So I blurted out the truth. "A client got a little rough last night."

The look on his face turned ferocious and he dropped his hand from my arm. *Shit.* Definitely not happy. I guess that was that. I'd be hearing about this from Sylvia when he called to complain. Just what I needed. Not to mention the money I *wouldn't* be bringing home with me tonight.

"Why would a man do such a thing?" he asked with a lethal edge to his voice.

I shrugged, trying to play it off. "It happens from time to time." His eyes narrowed and my gaze darted away from his face.

"Bastardo!" he roared.

Usually when I was with one of my clients, I felt like I held all the power. Marco had barely touched me, yet it somehow felt like he was the one with the power. And that set me on edge.

I wrapped my arms around myself and clutched at my upper arms, unsure what to make of his reaction.

"I have frightened you," he said in a softer voice. The

look on his face transformed into one of repentance rather than anger.

"I...I don't understand why you're so upset, that's all."

"Is it acceptable in your country for a man to lay his hands to a woman?"

"Well, no. But I'm not exactly an innocent here, Marco."

"It should matter not what you do for a living. You are still a woman, are you not?"

I ignored the tug in my chest over the fact that he'd been upset by another man's mistreatment of me and reached for my purse to return his money. "I understand if you'd prefer to cancel our plans this evening—"

"Nonsense." Marco's grabbed my purse and set it back down on the table.

"You're sure?"

His gaze roamed my face and he was silent for a moment before he gave me a quick nod.

"Thank you." I drew in a deep breath and mentally shook off the disappointment I'd felt a moment before.

"Why don't we discuss what I have planned for this evening?"

"Terrific. What did you have in mind?" I asked.

"You'll be accompanying me to an event."

That was...unexpected. It wasn't the first time a client had wanted me to escort him to an event, but it wasn't a regular occurrence. Most men were more interested in getting me naked. "How long is this event?"

I was used to being out all hours of the night, but I had to be home well before Daniel woke up.

"I am a very wealthy man, Brandi." Marco said my name with a look of disgust as if it tasted foul on his tongue.

"Money is no object. We will leave when I've accomplished what I've set out to do…and not before."

The authority in his voice came naturally to him; that much was obvious. Given the fact that he could afford my hourly rate, I assumed he was a man who was used to people following his orders without question.

"You know it's extra for me to escort you to an event?" I questioned.

He nodded. "I've spoken to Sylvia about it."

I shrugged. It was all the same to me. As long as I left here with a purse full of cash, I'd be a happy hooker. "When do we leave?" I asked with a smile.

"I must finish getting ready. Make yourself at home, and I'll be back in un momento."

I watched as Marco stalked toward the master bedroom with the energy of a caged animal. The man was intense, but even when he didn't seem to be trying, I could see the simmering energy beneath the surface. I'd bet that he was the kind of person who captured everyone's attention when he walked into a room.

I glanced around the space, trying to get any kind of read on the man I'd be spending the evening with. There were no personal items to be found. I had no idea how long he'd been in town before I met him a few days ago, but if you were to look around, you wouldn't know someone was staying here.

Since that was a bust, I fished my phone from my clutch and texted Leroy to let him know that I'd be accompanying Marco off the premises. Leroy would make himself scarce, but he'd follow us wherever we were going. His job was to look out for me, but not at the expense of making clients feel like he was breathing down their necks.

As I was checking my email on my phone a few minutes later, a tingling sensation along my spine alerted me to Marco's return. "Are you ready to depart?" he asked with that Italian accent that was beginning to do funny things to my insides.

I inhaled a deep breath and turned to face him. "Ready and willing..." The words died on my tongue as I took in his appearance. He'd buttoned up his white shirt and now wore a charcoal three-piece suit that stretched across his broad chest. Damn it, the man looked so fucking edible I was forced to clench my thighs together. "We still need to discuss the specifics of my payment for the evening."

His dark eyes narrowed. "Yes, we do." He placed both his hands in his pockets and stood with his legs spread. I couldn't help but notice the bulge between his legs.

I squared my shoulders, ready to upsell my little ass off. "I have to admit that I'm a little out of my element. I'm not normally negotiating an evening's festivities when I have no idea what they entail."

High-end hooking was all about the upsell. You wanted sex without a condom? Extra. You want me to swallow? Extra. Have a penchant for ass play? Extra.

He stood silent and unblinking for a moment. It unnerved me the way he seemed to always be sizing me up. "Will ten thousand dollars cover our time together?"

I almost choked on my tongue. *Ten thousand?* I made good money on any given night, but this would be the most I'd ever made in a night—and I wasn't even sure I was going to have to sleep with the guy.

"Um...that should be fine." I attempted to give the air that I was paid that much all the time, but I wasn't sure I succeeded. Even with the cut I'd have to pay Sylvia, I was still in record-breaking territory. It gave me new strength to deal with my apparent attraction to the man in front of me.

"I can retrieve it for you now if you like." He dipped his head, looking at me from under his brows.

"I'd appreciate that."

He left for the bedroom and returned a moment later with a small wad of cash, which I took from him and added to the one already in my purse.

"Thank you."

He nodded and pulled a phone from his pocket, fingered a few keys, and raised it to his ear.

"Siamo pronti ad andare," he said and flipped the phone closed. "My driver will meet us downstairs."

I picked my purse back up from the table. "I'm ready."

"Ladies first," he said, gesturing for me to head out the door in front of him. As my designer stilettos clicked on the marble floor beneath me, it was as if his gaze penetrated the expensive fabric draped over my body. I dressed the part of a high-priced escort, but I was the only one who knew that the majority of my evening attire came from second-hand stores or discount websites.

I continued to walk in front of him doing my best to appear unaffected. Though I was used to having my body ogled by men—in fact, I dressed to encourage it—something about the way Marco looked at me left me unsettled. Even when I wasn't able to see him doing it.

When we reached the main level of the hotel and exited the doors, there was an older gentleman standing beside a black Escalade with dark tinted windows. He nodded his head at us when Marco caught his eye.

"This way." Marco glanced around as we walked to

the vehicle. "Sal, this is Brandi." He motioned between the two of us. "Brandi, Sal."

I put my hand out to shake, and Sal took it in his. He had streaks of grey through his hair and wore large rings on his fingers that bit into my skin when he shook my hand. He appeared to be in his mid-fifties.

"Pleasure," he said, unsmiling, with the same accent Marco possessed.

"Sal has worked for my family for many years." Sal opened the door and Marco placed his hand on my back, applying a light pressure so I would climb into the vehicle.

I did so, careful not to rip the seams in my dress, and settled in the far seat. Marco slid in beside me, the scent of his expensive cologne filling the small space. Our legs weren't touching, but we were close enough that I felt the heat of his warm body drawing me toward him. I shifted my legs in the opposite direction.

Sal strode around the front of the car and got in the driver's seat, immediately pulling away from the curb.

"Where is it we're headed?" I wanted to be able to prepare for what lay ahead.

"Tonight, we'll be attending a party. There will be someone there I'm hoping to do business with."

Well, that was vague. "And what exactly is your business?" I knew better than to ask too many questions—especially in Vegas—but a part of me wanted as much information as I could get about the mysterious Marco Valenti.

"My family owns many companies."

"Okay then." I was unable to help the irritation that crept into my voice. I don't know why I felt that way—I had no right. Marco could tell me as much or as little as he chose.

He was the one paying, so he called the shots.

He frowned for a moment then seemed to resign himself to something based on the heavy sigh that escaped his lips. "I'm in America to secure a location for our newest hotel and casino. Valenti Enterprises has luxury properties all over the world."

Wow. So not only did he come from money, he came from *money*. "And what is it you'd like me to do this evening…smile and look pretty?"

His gaze roamed over my body and back up again. I stole a quick glance in Sal's direction.

"Don't worry about Sal. He's completely trustworthy. Are you?"

"P…pardon?" I stammered, surprised by the change in topic.

"Are you trustworthy?"

"I get paid to keep secrets, Marco."

The cold, assessing eyes that had been staring me down warmed a bit with my answer, and the corner of his mouth twitched. I had the impression that my client was amused by my cheekiness.

We traveled in silence for a while longer while I replayed my time in his hotel room over and over again in my head, wondering what it was about this man that was getting to me.

Marco shifted in his seat to face me. "When we arrive, I want you to only speak when spoken to and offer no information about yourself. People are to think you are my date and not…"

He trailed off but didn't appear to be the least bit chagrined about what he'd almost said.

"A hooker," I finished for him.

His mouth set in a thin line. "I prefer the term *escort*. After all, that is what you're doing this evening...escorting me to a function."

"I suppose." I shrugged. "Who will be at this soirée?"

"People I'm hoping to do business with."

Oh good. Glad he cleared that up.

We rode the rest of the way in comfortable silence. Twenty minutes later, we pulled up in front of a sleek-looking white stucco building with large glass windows. It wasn't a residential building, but there was no sign overhead to signify exactly what it was. While I was curious why we were here, I didn't question Marco. I was being paid to do what he asked of me, and apparently that meant acting like silent arm candy for the evening.

Worked for me. I could certainly smile and nod for ten large. Hell, I'd be stupid not to. It put me one step closer to my ultimate goal, and then I'd be able to do something with my life that I'd actually be able to share with my son.

CHAPTER SEVEN

I held my breath as we stepped through the glass doors of the building, unsure what to expect on the other side since all I was able to see was a reflection of the outside world. When I got a view of the room in front of me, I exhaled a relieved breath.

We were in an art gallery.

Large abstract paintings splashed with bright colors hung on the walls. A few dozen or so people admired the works of art with champagne glasses in their hands.

Marco led me further into the room with his hand placed on the small of my back, his thumb tracing an invisible path along my spine as he moved it back and forth.

To anyone else we probably looked like a couple well acquainted with each other, which couldn't be further from the truth. I knew nothing about Marco Valenti, and he certainly knew zip about me.

"Care for some champagne?" His deep voice rumbled as he bent down to speak into my ear. A shiver ran up my spine, and because of where his hand was, he noticed.

His gaze caught and held mine for a moment. Then we both looked at the waiter who'd stopped in front of us holding a tray with champagne flutes.

I reached for one and smiled. "Thank you."

Marco did the same but skipped the formalities. He was already assessing the crowd—who he was looking for, I had no idea.

I lifted the flute to my lips and took a small sip. The bubbles broke on my tongue and the sweet taste of the liquid spread throughout my mouth. No surprise that it wasn't the cheap stuff.

"So what is this place?" I asked in a hushed tone so only Marco would hear me.

He raised a brow. "Isn't it obvious?"

"Clearly, it's an art gallery of some kind, but there was no sign outside. How are people supposed to know what it is so they can come in and check it out?"

He gave me a sideways smile as he looked down at me. "Places like this don't need to advertise, and they certainly don't want foot traffic. This is by invite only."

"Oh." My face heated in embarrassment. I had no idea such places even existed.

Marco led me to stand in front of a large canvas that had bright orange and yellow streaks across it with one small black square in the corner. Frankly, it didn't look like much to me, but then again, what did I know? I was sure I couldn't have afforded even the tiny black square on the canvas.

"How did whoever runs this place know you were in town if you only just arrived?" I took another sip of my champagne.

Marco turned in my direction, once again assessing

me with those dark eyes of his. "What makes you think I've only just arrived? I said no such thing."

"The hotel room didn't appear to be lived in. There were no dirty glasses or anything on the bar when you made yourself a drink, and the remotes for the TV were arranged on the coffee table like a maid would do. In fact, not one single thing was out of place in the entire room. I know it's a high-end hotel, but if you'd had time to relax there even a minute, then a pillow would have been moved on the couch or a stray receipt would've ended up somewhere on one of the tables."

His eyes widened, and for a moment he appeared unsettled. "You got all that from being in my hotel suite for such a short time?"

Thinking maybe I had overstepped, I shifted on my feet and looked back to the painting. "It's no big deal. In my line of work, you have to assess a place quickly when you enter it. Know what you're getting into."

"Sei intelligente come sei bella."

I turned to look at him. I had no idea what he just said, but the words sounded beautiful tumbling from his lips. "In English, please?"

He leveled me with a stare that I felt down in my soul. How that was possible without even knowing him at all, I had no idea, but I was locked in place by the weight of his stare, the same as if my ankles had been bound in lead shackles. "I said, you are as smart as you are beautiful." Marco brought a hand up to caress my cheek, not breaking eye contact.

I held my breath.

He dropped his hand and turned back to the canvas. "I made sure the owner knew I was in town and looking for a new piece to add to my collection."

I blinked a few times, trying to keep up. "I see."

At that moment, an attractive older woman sidled up next to Marco. She wore a fitted royal blue dress over her willowy frame. It showcased just enough cleavage to make a man look, but not so much that she appeared sleazy. Her blonde hair was cut in a severe bob just past her chin, and I'd guess her to be in her late thirties.

She smiled at us both. "It's really something, isn't it?"

"Sì. The way he's thrust the paint on the canvas with such abandon and the juxtaposition of the black square...it's stunning," Marco responded.

"Alexa Sands." She put her hand out to shake Marco's. He took it from her and brought it to his lips, giving it a quick peck like he'd done to me a few times. My chest constricted when Marco's lips met her skin, but I ignored the disappointment I felt at the reminder that there was nothing special between us.

"Marco Valenti," he replied and then motioned toward me. "This is Brandi."

I inwardly grinned that he'd left off a last name. Brandi didn't have a last name.

"Pleasure to meet you," I said, smiling.

She spared me a quick glance but otherwise seemed taken by the charming smile Marco had plastered on his face. The two of them carried on a conversation about the art and the artist, to which I had nothing to offer, so I politely excused myself to visit the restroom. Marco and Alexa barely noticed when I departed.

I tried to keep my head down as I made my way through the crowd on the off chance that I ran into someone I knew. Not anyone in my personal life, because I didn't have one. In fact, I'd made a point to never have friendships outside of work to avoid any questions. My nights were spent in sin and my days were spent with my son.

No, I was worried about seeing one of my other clients. Marco had made it clear that he didn't want anyone here to know he was paying for my company, and I wasn't about to fuck up my big payday.

I reached the bathroom without incident, and since I was alone, I pulled my phone from my purse to make sure I didn't have any messages from Martina.

Nothing.

Relief eased some of the tension in my shoulders. Everything must be okay with Daniel. Even then, I knew how quickly things could go from good to bad with a child in his condition, so worry was never far from my mind.

The only number that appeared on my phone was from Vivian. She ran another escort agency in town and had been trying to poach me from Sylvia for a long time. It didn't seem to matter how many times I told her I wasn't going anywhere, she continued to pester me to turn my back on Sylvia.

And that was something I couldn't do. Sylvia rescued me from a bartending job at a strip club that was going nowhere fast and took me under her wing. She groomed me into a high-end escort who commanded thousands of dollars from men for a few hours' work. If it weren't for Sylvia, I wouldn't be able to pay for all of Daniel's medical bills and therapies. And I certainly wouldn't have a chance in hell of achieving my dream.

I deleted the message without listening to it. I was loyal to Sylvia. It would take hell freezing over to change that. After I returned my phone to my purse, I primped in front of the mirror and made my way back out to the party.

As I approached, I saw Alexa laughing at something Marco had said. She placed her hand on his upper arm while he graced her with a thousand-watt smile that implied that he was enjoying the attention. Not at all understanding the purpose of my presence here, I saddled back up to the two of them, clicking my heels a little harder than necessary.

They both turned in my direction, and Marco cast me a subdued version of the smile he'd given Alexa. Then he passed me back my champagne and wrapped his arm around my waist as he'd done earlier.

"You'll never believe it," he said with a casualness to his voice I didn't believe for a second. "Alexa here is part of the land development committee with the city."

My thoughts traced back to his earlier admission that he was in Vegas to secure a spot for a new casino. "You don't say," I replied, playing along.

"I was explaining to her how my company is getting ready to submit a proposal for the demolition and re-zoning of one of the local city-owned properties."

I smiled, not sure what else to do. I needn't have worried about that, because apparently Alexa knew *exactly* what needed to be done.

"Why don't we schedule some time together?" Alexa's words dripped with innuendo, but I pretended not to notice. "I can take a look at your preliminary proposal and tell you if I think you'll run into any trouble. Maybe give you a few suggestions as to what might help you get it past the committee."

"Grazie. That would be most kind of you." He tipped his head down at her and reached for her hand, squeezing it.

Alexa's hand slinked forward and squeezed Marco's forearm. "It's no trouble, I assure you." God, this woman was practically eye-fucking him right in front of me.

Marco reached for something inside his pocket, forcing Alexa to drop her hand. Just as well before I ripped it from her body and beat her with the bloody stump.

I needed to get a grip. This was just another job. It shouldn't matter that the man was entirely too attractive for his own good.

"Here's my card." Marco held a glossy black business card out to her.

She took it, inspecting it for a moment before putting it in her clutch. "Wonderful. I'll call you later this week and we can set something up. It's been great chatting with you, Marco."

"Likewise, Alexa." Marco gave her a dazzling smile that even I had a hard time not being affected by.

"Brandi." She nodded her head at me in a dismissive way before moving on to a painting located on the other side of the room.

Marco said nothing but sidestepped over to the next painting. I followed suit and sidled up to him again like we were lovers. "Should I bother asking how a woman who works for the city, making a city salary, has enough money to get invited to an event like this?"

His jaw tensed. "In gamba." He paused then translated for me, "Probably not." Raising the glass to his lips, he took a sip of his champagne. For some reason I couldn't understand, I found myself wondering what it would be like to kiss him. Granted, kissing was all part of the program, but I'd never *wanted* to kiss a client before.

Shaking my head slightly, I shifted my body away from him, needing a break in our physical connection. Marco stopped me by reaching for my free hand and linking it with his.

"It's not what you think. At least, not for me." He'd mistaken my separation for dislike over the fact that he'd been speaking with a city official that, if I had to guess, accepted bribes.

In reality, I didn't care what he was into. It made no difference in my life as long as I was safe while I was with him and was paid for my time. What I cared about was why I found myself even the slightest bit attracted to him. And what puzzled me more was why he'd even care what I thought about any of it.

CHAPTER EIGHT

An hour later Marco and I stood in front of the only painting we hadn't yet seen, and it was the first one I was really taken with. Unlike most of the other paintings on display, the colors on this canvas were muted. The artist had used mostly black and gray, and only the slightest bit of color peeked through where it had been swirled in with the darker colors.

"You enjoy this one." Marco turned and faced me with a soft smile on his face.

I nodded, unable to deny it. He brought his hand up to my face and pushed a tendril of hair behind my ear.

"Falling for art can be like falling for a person," he said. "Sometimes you're drawn to it for reasons you can't comprehend. It's either suited to you, or it's not. Once discovered, it can be difficult to pull your gaze from its beauty."

I held his stare for a long moment as my vision—my entire consciousness—tunneled to one thing: Marco. The murmurs of people around us and the combined scent of expensive colognes and perfumes faded away as I stood transfixed.

Eventually, Marco's attention shifted back to the art and I followed suit. The plaque underneath said the piece was titled *Emergence*.

On a hunch, I stepped back several feet, stopped for a moment to look at the canvas, and then backed up several more feet.

Ah, there. I was right.

Once I'd moved far enough away from the canvas, a pattern emerged. It hadn't been obvious at first because the canvas was so large and we'd been so close, but now it was clear that all of those seemingly random swirls and swipes of paint formed an intentional design.

My gaze darted to Marco, whose brows were furrowed, and I motioned him over to where I stood. I couldn't help noticing the way the muscles in his arms and thighs flexed underneath the fabric of his suit as he approached. Then I reminded myself—again—that I shouldn't be noticing those things.

"Why did you come all the way over here?" he asked.

"See for yourself." I gestured to the painting behind him.

He turned to take in the painting and his dark eyes lit with amusement, a small smile playing on his face. "How did you know this?"

"The title—*Emergence*." He raised a brow, so I continued. "'Emergence' can mean a few different things, but it usually refers to when larger patterns arise through the interaction of smaller entities." Marco looked like I'd confused him more than ever. "Think of a snowflake or a flock of birds...a school of fish, perhaps. A pattern exists in those complex structures. If you were to look at a snowflake closely, it would just look like random lines spiking in every direction. But take a look from farther away and you can see how all those pieces organize themselves to form a pattern, even though at first it seemed random and unorganized."

Understanding lit Marco's face and he smiled down at me. "I've never heard of such a thing."

"The idea itself has been around for centuries. Some philosophers believe that if humanity were left to its own devices, society wouldn't devolve into a state of chaos but that we'd regulate ourselves and spontaneous order would arise." I smiled at Marco, enjoying the opportunity to have an adult conversation for a change. With very few friends and most of my working hours spent on my back or on my knees, the opportunity didn't present itself often.

He set his empty champagne glass on a passing waiter's tray, then shoved his hands in his pockets. "And do you believe this theory?"

Skipping briefly over the memories of all I'd seen and experienced, I sighed. "No. I think most people would think only of their own agenda. In the end, only the strong would survive and they'd impose their will on others."

"Survival of the fittest." He nodded, his eyes serious.

"That's been my experience." I drew the last sip from my champagne flute and savored the sweet liquid as it ran down my throat. Spotting a waiter a short distance away, I excused myself to deposit the empty glass on his tray, happy to be out from under Marco's keen assessment for a moment.

"Thank you, miss," the waiter said with a lecherous look on his face. He used the opportunity to take a quick inventory of my assets. *Gross.* With a shiver of revulsion worming its way up my spine, I turned to head back over to Marco just as the door to the gallery opened behind him.

The man who stood there had me wide-eyed and frozen in fear.

CHAPTER NINE

Everybody knew who Vito Manzella was.

At least everyone who worked on the wrong side of the law did.

Vito had his hand in a lot of shady dealings in Vegas. I wouldn't exactly use the word 'mob boss' to describe him, but suffice it to say he was a man you did *not* want to fuck with.

He'd been in Las Vegas for decades, and word from other working girls was that he was into some weird shit. If he took a liking to you, you were stuck with him until he was done with you. I'd heard that a couple of women had been forced to deal with his mistreatment and sick demands for upwards of a year before he tired of them.

The last thing I wanted was to attract his attention. There was nothing about me this evening that screamed 'high-end call girl,' but nothing good could come from landing on his radar.

Vito walked in like he owned the place, and it was

very likely he did. In person, the man was only a little taller than me, with a protruding belly and slicked back gray hair. He was flanked by two large men sporting similar hairstyles, minus the gray.

He took a quick look around and his face lit with recognition when he spotted Marco. *Damn.* He headed in his direction. Vito must've seen Marco watching me because his gaze darted over to me and the corners of his lips tilted up into a sinister smile. *Double damn.*

Pretending I didn't notice, I started walking again until I'd reached Marco, embracing him when I did. I'd give Vito no reason to suspect that Marco and I were anything other than lovers. I could only hope Marco would do the same.

I also prayed he didn't say anything to put him on Vito's bad side. Why I cared about Marco's well-being was beyond me, but the fact was that he had treated me with a great deal of respect thus far.

A smarmy grin spread across Vito's face as he reached a hand out to Marco. "Buonasera."

Marco's jaw ticked before he took his hand. With a curt nod, he said, "Vito."

How well did they know each other?

"Fellas," Vito said, glancing from one beefcake at his side to the other. "This is Carmine's son." The satisfied and knowing grin that spread across Vito's wrinkled face unsettled me.

Marco's muscles tensed beneath my hand. I had no idea why, but the hair on my arms stood on end. Instinctively, I rubbed my hand up and down Marco's back in a soothing gesture. He recovered quickly, putting on a practiced smile then gesturing to me. "This is Brandi."

I reached my hand forward to shake Vito's, and he immediately pulled it up to his mouth and placed a kiss on it. I resisted the urge to wipe my hand against my expensive dress to remove the small amount of saliva left over from his lips. Vito's dark eyes looked me up and down with no hurry before he said, "É molto bella." His gaze darted over to Marco and he nodded his head. "Bravo."

It didn't take a genius to figure out that bella meant beautiful and I repressed the urge to shudder.

"I heard that you might be in Vegas," Vito said, steepling his hands in front of him. "What brings you here?" Vito still had his Italian accent, but it wasn't as thick as Marco's.

Marco responded in his mother tongue. He and Vito then spoke rapid-fire Italian to each other, none of which I understood. But I didn't need to. Their body language told me that they were sizing each other up. And though the conversation didn't sound heated, there was an underlying tension below the public display of civility that radiated off our small group like an invisible shockwave from an atomic bomb.

When they were finished with their conversation, both men leaned in and did the double-kiss-on-the-cheek thing as if they were the best of friends. *Right, and I was going to join a convent tomorrow.*

"We must be leaving." Marco tipped his head to the men and then gripped my hand tightly in his own. "Enjoy the art."

I followed behind with him practically dragging me out of there. I glanced over my shoulder as we exited through the door to see Vito looking after us with narrowed eyes that reminded me of a snake's.

Though I'd love to question Marco as to his relationship with Vito, I knew my place. And it wasn't to go nosing into my client's business, so I remained silent until Sal pulled up to the curb and exited to open the door for us. He glanced quickly behind us, eyes alert and assessing.

Marco's warm hand fell to my back and guided me into the back of the vehicle. We sat in silence as Sal returned to the driver's side and then pulled the car away from the building.

I gazed out at the bright lights of Vegas as the car whizzed by one casino after another. I'd always found it ironic how the dazzling lights of this city hid such an undercurrent of corruption and despair.

Marco squeezed above my knee to get my attention, and I startled. "The emergence aspect of that piece...how did you know to view the painting from farther away?"

My stomach turned as I tried to quickly figure out a way to play off his question. My fascination with the piece had overwhelmed me, and I'd let my guard fall for a split second. A couple of sentences and already he was asking questions about the *real* me.

I shrugged. "Just did." His jaw clenched, and before he could say anything further, I tried changing the subject. "Do you want to discuss what you'd like to do when we get back to the hotel?"

The thought of being intimate with Marco made me nervous, but for reasons other than the usual ones.

"Do not do that," he snapped.

"Do what?" I asked, trying to appear oblivious.

He squeezed my leg again, and I resisted the urge to push my thighs together. *The feel of his hands on me...*

"You know exactly what. Now answer my original

question." He pinned me with an intense gaze, and my reaction was the same as if he were holding me down—I was unable to move, transfixed by his stare.

I swallowed hard before answering. "College classes."

"You are a student?" He raised a brow. I guess he'd never heard of working your way through college.

"I take some online classes," I replied, shifting in my seat.

Marco seemed to ponder that information for a moment before responding. "What is it you take?"

This conversation was venturing into territory I wasn't comfortable with. Never before had I divulged *any* information to a john. My work and home life had always been completely separate, which was how I liked it. My clients paid a lot of money to see me cast in whatever role they wanted. Blurring the lines between the real me and the fictional one I'd created wasn't an option. That said, I wanted to keep this man happy—and I sure as hell wanted to keep the ten thousand dollars.

"Brandi. I asked you a question." Marco's low timber dragged me from my thoughts.

Picturing the excitement in my son's eyes when he saw the building, I answered Marco honestly. "I took some philosophy classes as electives for the degree I'm working on. Not a big deal."

Marco raised his eyebrows. "That shows initiative."

Maybe it did, but it wasn't the reason I took them. I never wanted my son to look at me with anything other than pride. If he knew what I did for a living in order to give him the best fighting chance, it would destroy him. And me. I had bigger dreams than lying on my back for the rest of my working life.

"Let's not talk about this." I slid closer to Marco on the leather seat. "There must be something else you'd rather discuss." I placed my hand above Marco's knee and then ran it up his inseam until my pinkie finger ever so gently brushed up against his sac.

He squeezed his eyes shut, almost as if he were in pain. I grinned to myself, thinking I'd successfully distracted him.

"Ho ricevuto un messaggio mentre eri dentro. Ti aspetterá davanti all'hotel," Sal interrupted from the front seat, earning a dirty look from me.

A split second later, Marco's large fingers wrapped around my wrist and removed my hand.

"What are you doing?" I asked, perplexed at why this man hadn't yet taken what he was owed.

"We will meet at the same time tomorrow night," he said between gritted teeth. "Dress for dinner."

The car pulled up in front of the Bellagio and a valet immediately opened our door. I hesitated before taking his hand and stepping out of the car. Marco was quick to follow.

I noticed Leroy pull up a few cars behind the vehicle we'd just exited. Shit, I'd forgotten all about him. That was a first.

"You can arrange it with Sylvia."

To my surprise, Marco brought his thumb to my chin in a gesture that felt almost sweet. "I will take care of her. Be sure you're on time."

I nodded, unsure what to make of Marco Valenti. He'd paid a large sum to have me on his arm tonight, and the fact that he didn't want to use my body was as foreign as he was.

Marco's thumb continued to press on my chin until

my mouth was forced to open. He gently pushed his thumb past my lips, and instinct had me wrapping my mouth around his digit. He exhaled on a small puff of air before he dropped his hand.

"Until then." He lifted my hand and kissed my knuckles before slowly returning my hand to my side. It tingled where he'd placed his lips. Without another word, he turned, putting his hands in his pockets. Then he said something to Sal in Italian before walking through the revolving doors into the lobby.

Before I went to say goodnight to Leroy, my gaze locked with a middle-aged man in a brown suit who stood watching me through the glass of the hotel lobby. He diverted his attention away from me once Marco made his way inside. Though he didn't say anything to Marco or Sal as they passed, he did turn to follow them.

I wasn't sure what was going on, but it was clear that I was wading into murky waters, and regardless of the smooth surface, there was something menacing lingering below.

CHAPTER TEN

"I don't trust this guy," Leroy grumbled as we walked down the hallway toward Marco's suite the following night.

I glanced to my side. "Why do you say that?"

"Ain't normal for no man to pay what he's paying and not wanna sleep with you."

I hadn't divulged my activities with Marco the night before, but Leroy was paid to notice details.

I shrugged. "Maybe he's just lonely." Leroy rolled his eyes and I had to agree. With the way Marco looked, if he was lonely, it was by choice. I had no doubt that we'd get to the sex part, but I was as surprised as Leroy that it hadn't happened on our first couple of nights together.

I inhaled a deep breath and tried to suppress the anticipation growing inside at seeing Marco again. Leroy rapped harder than necessary on the suite's door, and I looked over at him with a small grin.

"What?" He held his hands up and there was an innocent expression on his face. I shook my head at him, amused.

Marco answered the door wearing a broad grin and another navy suit, only this one had the faintest blue pinstripes through it. He'd shed the jacket at some point and wore only the vest, and his biceps noticeably strained the fabric on the arms of his pale blue dress shirt.

"Brandi." He nodded at me then regarded Leroy for a moment, but he didn't say anything to him. "You look lovely as always. Please, come in. I thought we'd dine in my suite."

This was more like it. This was what I was used to. He probably wanted to eat here so we didn't waste any time before he got me flat on my back—or on my knees. More likely, both.

"Of course." I gave him my practiced smile, the one I'd perfected on many a man before him, and stepped into the room. Then I nodded at Leroy before closing the door behind me.

The scent of fresh flowers filled the suite as I strolled into the main living/dining area. Arrangements full of all white flowers were perched on various surfaces throughout the living room. The table had been set for formal dining and music played softly in the background.

Opera. *Interesting choice.*

"Would you care for a drink?" Marco stood with his hands in his pockets, legs spread apart. I couldn't help but think how much he looked like a male model in a clothing ad. His dark, assessing eyes took me in, but otherwise he appeared to be much more relaxed than he'd been the night before.

Until I opened my big mouth.

I needed something to dull the effect he had on me. "A gin and tonic, please."

Marco's eyes darkened. "That was my father's drink." His statement was delivered without inflection, and I was unsure how to respond.

"Are you two close?" I asked.

"No. He's dead." His lips pressed into a thin line.

If I'd been paying any attention at all, I'd have noticed he used *was* in his sentence, not *is*.

"I'm sorry," I whispered.

"It matters not." There was something there—a history of some kind with his father that seemed to be less than stellar—but I let the subject drop. I knew better than anyone what it was like to have a strained relationship with a parent. Or a non-existent one, in my case.

He took heavy steps to the bar and began mixing our drinks. I watched as his long, elegant fingers performed the task and wondered what else he could do with those hands.

When he was done, he made his way back over to me and handed me my drink with a smile on his face. Any trace of the discomfort I'd seen minutes before had vanished.

"A toast," he said, raising his glass. "To new adventures."

I clinked my glass with his. "To new adventures," I repeated, the image of the property I wanted to purchase flashing through my mind.

Taking a sip from the glass, I asked, "Will we be going anywhere tonight?"

He shook his head while pinning me with his dark chocolate eyes, an intense vibe rolling off him like waves that threatened to bowl me over. Slowly, he brought his glass to his lips and took a sip, appearing to be in no hurry at all. "We will spend the evening indoors."

He took in my appearance from head to toe, his gaze

lazily sliding up and down my body. It was difficult not to squirm under his intense inspection. My heart sped up a fraction of a beat, and I was unable to look away as I pondered what being with this man would be like. Strangely enough, I *wanted* to know. If I left here tonight not knowing what it was like to fuck Marco Valenti, I was going to be one very unhappy hooker.

I turned to look out the large windows and took a healthy sip of my drink, hoping the gin would wash away my inappropriate feelings.

After chatting for a few minutes, I began to relax. We spoke of nothing of consequence, but Marco was cordial if not charming, and some of his rough edge had dissolved.

He excused himself to the bar, where he poured himself another two fingers of whiskey. When he returned, I noticed that his aura had changed. The muscles in his face were drawn and his lips were pressed into a flat line.

"I want to discuss something with you, Brandi." His voice was serious, and I was on instant alert. What could he possibly have to discuss with me that would garner such a change in his demeanor?

Please don't let this guy be into some freaky shit.

"What is it you'd like to talk about?" I held my breath as I awaited his answer.

"I would like you to be available to me for the remainder of my stay."

I blinked several times. "What exactly does that mean...available to you?"

"I don't like to share. And I don't intend to. My schedule can change without notice and I'd like to know that, while I am here, if I call and request your presence, you will come."

Hearing the words *'you will come'* from Marco's mouth sent a chill down my spine that settled in a warm, tingling sensation in the center of my thighs.

Spending more time with Marco would be no hardship, though there was one huge problem. "That's an interesting offer, but I'm not available during the day."

"If I pay you, you will be." He pinned me with a stare that dared me to argue.

"That's non-negotiable," I responded, my voice firm.

He gave a caustic laugh. "Dolcezza, I think you forget who is in charge."

My face heated. "I said it's *not* negotiable."

He studied me for a moment, running his thumb along his bottom lip. *God, that was hot.* "Do I need to call Sylvia to discuss this?" *His passive-aggressive threat? Not so hot.*

I lifted my chin and put my hands on my hips before responding. "She'll tell you the same thing, I'm afraid." I met his gaze head-on, letting him know that I wouldn't back down.

"Fine," he ground out, but it was clear that he didn't like conceding. His fists were clenched at his sides.

"That means putting all of my other clients on hold." I crossed my arms in front of my chest. "You're going to have to make it worth my while."

"You...drive a hard bargain. Is that what you Americans say?" I gave a quick nod of my head. His mood had shifted and he smiled, but make no mistake, the curve of his lips still held a predatory edge. "I like it."

Marco put his hands in his pockets, all quiet confidence. "I'll pay you double what you would normally make an evening. But you must clear your calendar of all other clients until I say otherwise." He stepped forward and leaned into me. "*That* is non-negotiable."

Double my usual fee? Done. I smiled, more to myself than him. This would allow me to set aside even more money for the down payment of the center. "Well, Mr. Valenti, you have yourself a deal."

"Marco," he snapped.

I found that I quite liked agitating him. It proved that I could get under his skin as much as he'd gotten under mine. Though it felt dangerous—a lot like poking the bear.

A knock sounded at the suite door.

"That's our dinner." Marco strode to the door, his long legs taking him there in half the time it would have taken me. He looked as good from the back as he did from the front. His suit pants cupped his muscled ass, and his broad shoulders and lean hips gave him the perfect silhouette—raw, powerful and masculine. All things I'd quickly figured out that Marco possessed in abundance.

A hotel employee wheeled the tray into the suite and unloaded the contents onto the dining table. Marco tipped him, and the young man gave me a small smile before leaving the room.

"Shall we?" Marco motioned to the table. I strutted over to the table, my newfound pay raise putting me in an exceptionally good mood.

Unsure where to sit, I glanced around the table until Marco pulled out the chair to the left of the head of the table. It was an unnecessary yet much appreciated chivalrous act. I got the impression that these small, seemingly insignificant gestures weren't "acts" at all, rather an innate part of who he was.

Taking my seat, I thanked him as he pushed my chair in closer to the table then took his seat at the head. It suited him. He looked like a powerful king as he surveyed the food in front of us.

"I hope you enjoy Italian food. It's not nearly as good as at home, but it will have to do."

"I do, thank you," I replied while placing my napkin in my lap.

Marco did the same. "Would you like some wine with your dinner?" he asked as he picked up a bottle off the table.

"I'll finish my drink, thanks."

He poured a healthy amount into his glass and set the bottle back down on the table. "Please, help yourself." He was such a refined gentleman at times that it made the intense edge he sometimes displayed even more unsettling.

Pushing that thought from my head, I reached for a large bowl filled with ravioli, while Marco grabbed some of the caprese salad and added it to his plate.

"What part of Italy are you from?" I asked as I cut the large squares of pasta into something I could actually fit into my mouth.

"My family is from southern Italy."

"I've never been to Italy, but it looks gorgeous," I said.

"It can be." He nodded. "Like most things that are beautiful on the surface, there is always more behind the façade." He smiled, but it didn't reach his eyes. Before I could ask what he meant by that, he continued. "Perhaps you will go one day."

Not likely, but he didn't need to know that. Traveling away from Daniel's home base without access to all his doctors and therapists made me anxious, so we'd never ventured anywhere further than a day trip's distance. I shrugged. "Maybe."

We ate in silence for several minutes, the awkwardness growing with each bite. I didn't know what the problem was. I was normally so good at this stuff. It was one of the reasons my clients requested me.

As I chewed around a mouth-watering piece of cheese-filled ravioli, I searched my brain for anything to talk about but came up empty. Marco saved me the trouble.

"I trust Sylvia explained my preference for our"—he waved his hand in front of him like he was trying to think of the appropriate word—"activities?" He placed his fork beside his plate and reached for his glass, taking a sip but not removing his gaze from me for a moment. The weight of his stare pressed heavily on my chest.

"She did." Sylvia let me know that Marco had sent in his test results and was clean, and that mine had been sent over to him as well. We wouldn't be using condoms this evening.

"This meets your approval?" He cocked an eyebrow and slowly set his glass down on the table.

"It does." He continued to pin those fathomless dark eyes on my own, and I squirmed a bit under the attention. Everything about this man had me wired. He was a perfect gentleman—suave, sophisticated and thoughtful even—yet there was much more than the polished veneer.

He picked his fork back up and continued eating. The rest of dinner was more relaxed with the two of us easily exchanging small talk. As the evening wore on, I became more comfortable around him and felt less like it was my first day on the job.

When I'd had enough to eat, I placed my cutlery on my plate and leaned back against my seat.

"Would you like some wine?" Marco suggested.

"Of course."

Wine sounded *perfect*. I could use a little alcohol to inject some calm into my body. Now that dinner was finished, I knew we'd be moving on to the next part of the evening—the part where he got what he paid for.

Marco rose from his chair and moved to pull mine out for me, then held out a hand to help me up.

I shouldn't be nervous; it was something I'd done countless times. This was different though. I was attracted to Marco, drawn to him in some inexplicable way. It was unsettling, to say the least.

I just needed to remember that nothing about what we were doing here was real. The wining and dining was all part of a sham constructed so he wouldn't feel like he was paying for sex. But when you got down to it, he was. And I needed to remember that.

I walked into the living room, relaxing a bit as I watched Marco prepare our drinks.

"Here you are." Marco approached holding out a wine glass to me.

"Thank you." I immediately brought the glass to my lips and took a small sip. The sweet coated my throat, but I enjoyed it. "It's very good."

Marco's eyes seemed to drink me in as he looked at me over his own glass. I watched as his Adam's apple moved when he swallowed. It stunned me that something like that could be so sexy.

Reaching forward, he took my wine glass from my hand and set it on one of the side tables. Then he stepped forward, eating up the space between us until we were only inches apart. His expensive cologne did nothing to stop the arousal that began to buzz between my legs. It was a foreign feeling to me. Sure, I'd been aroused on some level before while I worked—though never enough to orgasm. And Marco not only aroused me physically but mentally as well.

It wasn't a welcome reaction.

I tried to think of unpleasant thoughts, anything to get me into the headspace where I was separated from my actions. But when he placed his hand on the side of my throat and ran his thumb up and down my pulse point, all the breath left my lungs. My nipples beaded underneath the fabric of my dress, and I stood waiting to see what he would do next.

His hooded gaze dipped down to my cleavage and continued south until it had feasted on all of me. Then Marco squeezed my neck slightly. Not so much that it was painful, but just enough to let me know the raw power he possessed.

I held my breath as he inched closer. Marco's lips were almost touching mine and his breath fanned across my face.

A phone rang from somewhere in the suite.

All the muscles in Marco's body stiffened. He squeezed his eyes shut for a moment before dropping his hand and stalking over to a nearby table to grab his phone.

He glanced at the caller ID and inhaled what appeared to be a calming breath before answering. "Ciao, Mamma." He held up a finger to me indicating that he'd be right back, and then he strode to the bedroom to take the call, closing the door behind him.

I let out a relieved breath.

What the hell was I thinking?

I hadn't been, obviously. I'd lost myself in him. There had been no escort and client, payer and payee—only pent-up lust demanding to be sated.

My lust.

CHAPTER ELEVEN

While waiting for Marco to finish up his phone call, I strolled over to the large window that looked down over the Bellagio fountains. I watched intently as cascades of sparkling water swayed back and forth, at times criss-crossing one another and other times shooting like rockets up into the air, only to fall back down moments later.

The artistic display continued as I tried to figure out how to keep Marco at arm's length. I needed him around because the money he was providing would help put me one step closer to making the center a reality. But the way that I was drawn to him scared me.

We were from two entirely different worlds that were as far apart as the two countries we each called home.

Nothing could ever come of us and there'd be no happy ending.

I was still deep in thought as the classical piece playing through the sound system finished and a new song began. The low notes of the piano keys seemed to echo through the room as if it were a vast cavern. Emotion welled up inside me as the haunting and mournful melody continued.

There was no room to let feelings develop in my line of work. Not lust, love, friendship, affection—none of it. This connection between Marco and me served as a reminder of all I was missing, of everything I could never, ever have.

"Scusa," Marco said as he entered the room from behind me. "A conversation with my mother is difficult to put to an end." I turned to face him and he stopped short. I smiled, but I knew it was a moment too late when he asked, "What is the matter?"

"Nothing," I answered quickly. "I've been listening to the music, watching the fountains. This song is so beautiful...and sad."

"It is indeed." He seemed to accept my answer.

Why wasn't I able to shut myself off around this man?

I tried never to think of what my life could have been like—there was no point. No one could turn back time, and besides, that would mean not having Daniel. That thought alone was enough to break me if I focused on it for too long.

But in that moment, sorrow gripped me and made me mourn for the woman I could've become had my life not veered off course at seventeen. Had I not believed a boy when he said he loved me.

"What's the name of this song?" I asked, my voice hoarse.

"Prelude in E Minor by Chopin."

I nodded and turned back to the windows. It meant nothing to me, of course. I didn't know the first thing about classical music, but I'd assumed—correctly—that with his sophistication and refinement, Marco would be familiar with the piece.

He walked up behind me. I couldn't see him, but I felt him draw near—that's how physically in tune I was to his body.

When he placed his hands on my shoulders and squeezed, I closed my eyes to prevent the sharp pricks I felt from becoming tears. I was unaccustomed to receiving any type of comfort from someone. I'd been on my own for so long, and in order to survive I'd had to harden myself, for both Daniel's sake and my own. Marco's hands provided a small measure of solace, and for this brief moment only, I'd allow him to soothe me.

"What saddens you, bella?"

I inhaled a deep breath to rein in my emotions before I twisted from beneath his gentle grip to face him. "I'm fine. Really." I smiled as best I could, willing the melancholy in my veins to melt away.

Marco's large hand settled on my face and he smoothed his thumb over my cheek. "That isn't so."

I looked him straight in the eye, urging him to believe me. "I promise. I'm fine. You don't need to be concerned."

"Of course I am concerned. You are here in my company." The look in his eyes said he was telling me the truth, but how could that be? Why was he acting like he cared at all about me when he'd paid me to sleep with him? Was this a game to him?

"I'm here because you're paying me," I bit out.

His muscles stiffened and Marco pressed his lips together. "Of that, I am fully aware." His hands dropped to his sides and his jaw ticked.

"I just meant..." I trailed off, unsure how to rectify the situation. I'd let my anger get the best of me. Marco looked into my eyes with such intensity in his dark gaze that I drew in a breath and held it.

Eventually, he wrapped his hands around me and I exhaled a shaky breath. He drew me to his firm chest and dropped his forehead to the top of my head. Being locked in his embrace and pressed against his body left me breathless. Tingling started in my extremities as Marco's hand caressed up and down my back. He nuzzled his face into my neck and drew in a deep breath, inhaling my scent.

"Profumi d'estate. You smell like a sweet summer breeze." His lips grazed my neck and I shuddered before he brought his forehead to mine.

His scent—a combination of expensive cologne with a hint of bergamot—drifted into my nostrils. Suddenly, I wanted to pleasure this man. Not because I was being paid to do it, but because I wanted him to want me, I wanted to make him happy, and I wanted to know him intimately. As fucked up as all that was.

I moved my hands to his chest, feeling his hard pecs flex beneath my palms as I dragged them down his abdomen, eventually lowering myself to my knees. The outline of his swollen cock was clear through his suit pants and I traced the shape with a single finger. When I reached the tip and squeezed, he hissed and pushed his hips forward. Wetness pooled between my thighs and my clit pulsed, demanding attention.

I looked up at him as I undid his belt and slowly pulled his zipper down. His large hands threaded into his hair, his eyes a little wild. My nipples hardened when I opened his pants and saw that he wore no underwear. *Did he always go commando?*

I licked my lips at the sight of his large, uncircumcised

cock, stiff and straining in front of me. Before I could act, Marco bent at the waist and reached down, gripping my wrists and stilling me. He squeezed them, and with only a look he told me to let go of his dress pants. I did, unable to help myself from doing his bidding.

Marco gently pushed one strap of my dress off my shoulder and then the other. He pulled the fabric down, and since I wore no bra, my breasts sprung free. His eyes flared and he bit down on his bottom lip, sucking it into his mouth as he did. Unable to control my reaction, my back arched, silently begging him to put his hands, mouth—hell, anything—on me.

My breasts felt swollen and heavy, my nipples almost painfully erect. Marco ran the back of his hand softly along the outside edge of one breast as my heart hammered in my chest like a tribal drum, the beat picking up speed the longer I was forced to wait. His heavy-lidded gaze drifted up to meet mine at the same time his fingers clamped around one of my nipples and squeezed. I cried out, my head dropping back at the pure ecstasy of pain that was matched with equal parts pleasure.

"Sei perfetta," he said, falling to his knees.

He palmed my breast, and I brought my head up just in time to watch his head dip down. He sucked the nipple he'd just delivered such exquisite torture to into his hot mouth, soothing the ache that remained. With no warning, he twisted my other nipple. My hands sprang into his hair while his steady gaze watched my reaction. His full lips dragged across my hot skin until he reached my other nipple and laved it, erasing the sting of his assault.

Then he squeezed both of my breasts, pressing them together. "I am going to fuck these beautiful tits. Soon."

God, I hoped Marco was a man of his word.

His stiff shaft bobbed with his movements while he played with me a little longer, sucking and pinching and pulling and tugging. Everything he did was driving me wild.

Finally, he pulled away from me and stood back up, his pants wide open and displaying his impressive manhood. Marco unbuttoned his vest and shirt as I kneeled below him, watching the buttons give way, one by one, revealing even more of his chiseled chest.

The man definitely spent time working on his physique. Starting at his protruding pecs, I reached up and ran my hands down his eight-pack and along the deep V carved into the lower half of his abdomen. Both the V and his dark treasure trail seemed to be pointing to the one thing that could ease the steady heat burning inside of me.

I hadn't realized how hard I was biting my bottom lip until Marco pushed his shirt off so that his cock was front and center, begging for attention. His dark, assessing eyes looked down on me, and a smug grin tugged on one corner of his mouth. "Open up, bella." His hand pushed into my hair and pulled me forward.

He didn't have to ask twice. I was more than happy to provide him with what he needed. This didn't feel like work, just want.

Pushing that thought to the back of my mind, my hand gripped the length of him and stroked. I teased him for a moment before finally wrapping my lips around the head of his cock.

Marco's hands tightened in my hair and he groaned. I swirled my tongue around and around his mushroom tip. His breathing picked up, but instead of giving him what he so desperately wanted, I allowed him to fall from my mouth.

His disappointment was clear from the sound of his groan, and I smiled. Gazing up at his heavy lids, I traced each side of his hard shaft with my mouth, gently nibbling as I went. I pushed my lips over the top of his bulbous head again, barely parting them and applying pressure at the same time. I did this a number of times, not allowing him to push himself into my mouth entirely.

"Play with your tits while you suck me." His voice was rough and his accent even more pronounced when he was turned on. It caused the heat between my legs to flare.

Instead of bringing my hand to my chest, I pulled his cock from my mouth and leaned back on my heels. He sucked in a breath and held it when he saw what I had in mind. With my hand positioned at the base of him, I traced the glistening tip of his cock around one of my nipples, then the other.

I moaned as his hot shaft brushed against my erect nipples. I flicked them back and forth, loving the tingling sensation that shot straight to my clit.

"Basta," Marco said, sounding as if he could explode at any moment. "Enough. Open that pretty mouth of yours."

I grinned and brought him back to my mouth, folding my lips around his cock and pushing forward until the tip of him reached the back of my throat. I wasn't able to take all of him in my mouth, but it was clear from his rapid breathing that I was driving him mad anyway.

I closed my eyes, but I could still feel Marco watching me from above. I pulled back and wrapped my lips over my teeth then pressed down as I moved back up his shaft. When I reached the tip, I swirled my tongue around a few times and his hands clamped harder in my hair.

I gradually increased my speed as I massaged his shaft

with my hands and ran my mouth up and down his length. He uttered Italian phrases that I couldn't decipher. It didn't matter. It was hot.

After a few minutes, one of my hands lightly grazed his large sac. A snarl ripped from Marco's throat, and he began thrusting himself into my mouth in earnest. As he face-fucked me, I moaned, loving that I was driving him wild. I glanced up at him to find him gazing down at me with eyes that appeared feral. He looked like a man beyond all reason.

Finally, he drove his cock into my mouth and held it there with a growl. His salty essence slid down the back of my throat and I drank him down. When he'd emptied himself, I pulled back, tucked his semi-erect shaft into his pants and zipped them up.

He helped hoist me to my feet, gripping my arms and dragging me to his chest. He gazed down at me, holding my stare as he always did, but there was a softness in his eyes that hadn't been present before.

I wasn't able to help the small smile that formed on my face. I felt more balanced. Like I'd taken back some of the power with our little exchange. Somehow I knew that Marco didn't allow other people to have power over him often, so it felt like a victory to me.

He watched intently as I pulled the straps of my dress back up my arms and readjusted the material so that my breasts were covered once again.

"Cosa mi stai facendo?" I looked at him in confusion, having no idea what he'd said. "What are you doing to me?"

Marco leaned in and brought his lips to mine. His were full and much softer than I expected them to be.

His tongue pushed against my lips for a split second before I reared back. "I'm sorry. We didn't discuss it, but I don't do that." I shook my head. "No tongue." It was too intimate. I needed to save something for myself.

It wasn't as if I'd have any suitors in lieu of the lifestyle I lived, but I'd always felt better knowing I'd held on to one small thing for myself. Most johns didn't care. They'd all rather have my lips wrapped around their cock anyway.

Marco dropped his hands instantly and took a step back, not saying a word, the stony exterior firmly back in place.

"I know, how very *Pretty Woman* of me." I laughed, trying to bring some levity to the moment, but the only change in Marco's demeanor was the crease between his brows. "*Pretty Woman*? It's an American film...with Richard Gere and Julia Roberts?" He continued to look at me like I had three heads. "Never mind," I muttered.

"I have an early meeting tomorrow. You should go."

I blinked a few times in shock. *He was kicking me out.* I guess hot millionaires didn't like to be told no. Especially when they were paying to assure themselves a yes.

"Okay," I said faintly. I straightened my dress and walked over to the table to collect my purse. When I held the small leather pouch in my hands, I turned back to look at Marco. "Thank you for a lovely evening."

He nodded, his expression devoid of feeling, but didn't say a word. Then he strode over to the bar and retrieved an envelope full of cash and held it out to me.

I pushed the envelope into my purse without checking to make sure it was the proper amount. "Okay then," I mumbled, feeling awkward. "Bye."

My heels clicked down the marble hallway as I made my way to the door. It hadn't escaped my notice that Marco didn't mention another date before he'd sent me on my way.

Great. I'd fucked up a steady paycheck—one that was *double* my regular fee—because I couldn't get past a little tongue. With all of the other things men did to me on a nightly basis, it seemed absurd. It probably was.

As I opened the door, the haunting notes of an opera floated from the speaker system, sounding every bit as tragic as I felt in that moment. I closed the door to the suite and, perhaps, the opportunity of a lifetime.

CHAPTER TWELVE

Daniel was resting after a long physiotherapy session this morning, so I'd taken the opportunity to catch up on my schooling. A steaming cup of tea warmed my hands while my eyes darted over the lecture in front of me.

My cell phone vibrated from where it sat beside my computer. I leaned forward to glance at the screen. *Sylvia*. I grabbed the phone and hit the round green button on the screen. "Hey, Sylvia."

"Hey, doll. How's it going?" she asked, her voice always rough and lower than you'd expect to hear from a woman.

"Pretty good. What's up?" I leaned back in my desk chair and twirled the mug in circles on the desk.

"I'm calling to give you a heads-up about something..." There was concern in her voice. I stilled, wondering what it could be. Had Marco called her about what had happened last night?

"Okay. What's going on?"

She sighed through the phone. "Julian's been calling for the last couple of days trying to book you for an evening. I've explained to him that you're off rotation for the time being, but he doesn't want to take 'no' for an answer."

"You didn't mention Mr. Valenti, I'm assuming?"

She guffawed. "Of course not. My ability to keep things quiet for our clientele is the only reason I'm still in business."

Sylvia was a vault. I should've known better than to even ask. "I'm not sure what you want me to say."

"Nothing, doll. I wanted you to be aware so that whenever the Italian Stallion is finished with you, you know where Julian's head is at."

My stomach contracted at the thought of Marco being *done with me*. Then I realized that her words also indicated that he wasn't—not yet anyway. So he hadn't called her to cancel our arrangement.

I sat up straight and cleared my throat. "Sure. Okay. Thanks for letting me know. Don't worry about Julian. I'll handle him whenever he books me next."

Julian was harmless—to me, at least. Yes, I had my suspicions as to how he made his money, but he'd never once been aggressive toward me. I was pretty sure it was a case of the male ego wanting what he couldn't have.

"I know you will. You're a professional." Sylvia hacked into the phone, years of smoking having taken their toll.

"You okay?" I asked.

"Don't you worry about me." She coughed again before continuing. "It's my job to worry about you girls."

That was one of the main reasons why I'd never turn my back on Sylvia. She'd taken me under her wing, showed me the ropes, and would never put me in a dangerous situation to make a buck. As odd as it seemed, she really did care for her girls.

"Well, someone has to watch out for you," I joked.

"I'm a tough old broad. Didn't make it this long not knowing how to take care of myself."

I laughed because it was true. Sylvia was no delicate flower.

"Thanks for letting me know about Julian. I'm sure he'll be fine. You know these big ego types with more money than sense. They don't like to be told no."

"Ain't that the truth."

We both laughed and caught up a bit before I returned to my coursework.

I sat in the chair in the corner of Daniel's room watching him sleep. If I didn't get him up soon, he'd never go to bed for Martina tonight.

When had my little boy grown up?

It seemed like yesterday that he was a toddler— learning new words, asking 'why' every five minutes, and devouring any and all attention he could get from his mommy. In fact, that was still how I envisioned him in my head sometimes.

These days, Daniel was all about owning his independence. It saddened me that he'd never really have it, but it wasn't pity I felt. Not even a little. That boy knew how to see the upside of almost any situation, and he *never* felt sorry for himself. I admired him for it.

He stirred in his bed a bit and I went to sit at the edge. "Hey, buddy," I said in a soft voice, running my fingers through his hair.

"Hey," he replied, his voice still groggy with sleep.

I glanced around the room, taking in the décor that had been there since he was much younger, and an idea took shape.

"I had a thought, and I want to see what you think of it." His eyes glimmered a bit, his interest in what I had to say evident. "What do you think about redecorating your room?"

A large smile spilled out over his face and reached into the deepest part of my soul like a soothing balm. "Really?"

I nodded. "You're getting older now. I think it's about time you had a say in what your room looks like."

Daniel's eyes sprung wide open, all vestiges of sleep now gone. "Mom, this is so awesome!"

I leaned forward and hugged him, willing the little boy in my arms to know how much he was loved. He returned the hug as best as he was able, and I exhaled a breath full of joy.

Moments like these were the best part of my day. The happiness Daniel brought into my life was infinite.

"We can head out to a few stores and see if there's anything you like," I said, already excited about this project we could work on together. "Oh, and we should grab some samples from the paint store, too."

"I want to paint the walls blue. Is that okay?"

I reached for his hand and squeezed it. "You can have whatever you want. Anything you want, it's yours."

There was truth in my words. I'd do whatever I could to make my son's life the best it could be.

CHAPTER THIRTEEN

It was a few days before Marco booked me again. Daniel and I had been busy collecting paint samples and visiting various stores and websites for different ideas. We'd even spent time on Pinterest, and I discovered that my son had more confidence in my crafting abilities than I did.

Still, my thoughts had drifted to Marco often. No matter how many times I checked my phone, there was still no word from the agency...until this afternoon.

Marco Valenti
9:00 pm
Meet him in front of Bobby's Room

It struck me as odd that he wanted to meet outside of the high-stakes poker room and not his suite, but I was beginning to realize that Marco wasn't like most johns.

Leroy met me right on time in the lobby of the north entrance. "Hey, baby girl. How's that little man of yours?"

I smiled at the mention of Daniel. "Getting older and wiser every day. Where does the time go?"

A sad smile crossed his face. "My momma used to say that one day she blinked and we were grown men." He rubbed a hand over the smooth dark skin on his bald head.

"You must miss her." Leroy's mom had passed away earlier that year, and he'd been deeply affected. I didn't know her, but they'd obviously been close based on how hard he'd taken her loss. It'd been almost a decade since I'd spoken to my own mother so I couldn't say I understood the feeling, but I still felt for my friend.

"Every minute of every day."

I reached around his sizeable waist and squeezed him tight. He placed one arm around me and hugged me back in return.

"Enough of this shit," he said, his voice gruff.

I pulled away and smoothed the front of my cream-colored silk dress. "You're right. I don't want to be late. I thought I'd screwed this up the last time I was with Mr. Valenti, and I don't want to press my luck."

We started on our way. "How'd you screw up?" he asked over the incessant ringing of the slot machines.

"Long story. But let's just say he didn't seem very happy with me when I left."

"I think that man'd have to be really pissed to cut ties with you."

I rolled my eyes at him. "Right," I said with an abundance of sarcasm.

"You seen the way he looks at you?"

I stopped short, almost causing the guy behind me to spill his drink all over my dress. *That was close.* He darted around us, and after getting a look at Leroy seemed to decide it wasn't worth cussing me out over.

"What do you mean the way he looks at me?" I asked.

"You blind, woman? That man wants you. Bad."

"They all want me, Leroy, what's your point?"

He shook his head slowly, his expression somewhat amused. "This is different, baby girl. Trust ol' Leroy on this one."

Could Leroy be right? And if he was, why did I feel almost giddy about it?

I shrugged and we continued on, side by side. I didn't have time to dig into my psyche at the moment.

A few bystanders watched intently as we walked by. I was pretty sure I *did* look like an escort at times like this—a curvy woman dressed to the nines with a hulking black man beside her. Either that or I looked like a celebrity who'd escaped LA and brought her bodyguard along.

As we passed one man with dark blond hair, I noticed he glanced a little too long at the pair of us. He seemed familiar to me, but I wasn't able to place him.

We reached the entrance to the high-stakes poker room, and it bothered me that I couldn't remember where I'd seen him before. But the longer I waited at the designated meet-up spot, the more irritated I grew that Marco was late and the less I thought about the mystery man.

I pulled my phone from my purse and saw that Marco was almost fifteen minutes late.

"You think he's not going to show?" I asked Leroy.

He gave a small laugh and looked at me like I was crazy. "What'd I tell you earlier? He'll be here."

I huffed out an aggravated breath. "I'm going to the ladies' room. You wait here in case Mr. Valenti does decide to show." My stomach dipped at the thought that maybe I wouldn't be seeing Marco this evening. I pushed that thought aside. I had to.

"Sure you don't want me to join ya?" Leroy's voice ripped me from my introspection.

I placed a hand on his hulking bicep. "I'm fine. I can make it to the restroom and back."

He shrugged and I left in the direction of the closest bathroom, walking along the path that wound around the outside of the casino area. The lights and bells on one of the slot machines to my right went off and cheers erupted from nearby patrons while I passed several restaurants on my left.

Leaving the restroom a few minutes later, I took the same path to return to Leroy, this time gazing at the people who were dining. Most of them were couples, probably here on vacation, taking a break from real life. This *was* my real life. Would I ever know what it felt like to be a part of a *real* couple? The question floated into my consciousness like a hot air balloon, but I refused to allow the idea to take flight.

That wasn't my life and probably wouldn't be for some time. My priority was my son. Still, a small, selfish part of me couldn't help but wonder what it would feel like to have someone love me—and to love them in return.

I stopped short when I saw a couple exit Le Cirque ahead.

Marco and Alexa.

It felt like a fist to the gut, pushing all the oxygen from my lungs, leaving only a burning sensation behind.

I watched as Marco led her out of the restaurant, and my gaze zoomed in where his hand was placed on her lower back. She was laughing at something he said, and I clenched my fists by my side as visions of punching that stupid grin off her face bombarded my mind.

They paused when they reached the path. I stood watching from a distance as they turned to face each other. I wasn't able to overhear what they were saying, but it clearly delighted Alexa—if the coy smile on her face was any indication.

I dragged a rough breath in through my nose and exhaled it through my mouth, doing my best to calm my racing heart.

Marco leaned in to kiss one of Alexa's cheeks and then the other, finally settling his lips on hers. It was a chaste kiss, but it lasted a little too long for my liking.

He pulled back and Alexa's hand rested on his face. She said something, leaned in to kiss him once more, and then finally made her way toward the main lobby.

Good thing, too, because I was seconds away from clawing her eyes out.

I needed to get a grip. Marco and I weren't lovers. He hadn't betrayed me. But then why did I feel this stinging sensation in my chest and the corners of my eyes?

"Aren't you supposed to be waiting for him by Bobby's Room?" The rich, Italian-accented voice came from behind me, and I spun to find Sal standing there. He looked none to pleased.

I hadn't realized just how intimidating he could be when we'd first met, but now with his hands crossed over his suited chest and his dark eyes boring into me, he seemed downright scary.

"I...I had to use the restroom."

"Sure you did." He looked over the top of my head and called out, "Marco!"

I glanced over my shoulder in time to see surprise flash in Marco's eyes when he caught sight of me, and for a moment I might have seen guilt as well. Then he stalked toward us—and stalked was the perfect description for it. He looked more like a panther sizing up its prey than a man approaching a woman.

"Brandi, why aren't you waiting where I instructed?" he bit out when he reached us.

"You were late, and I had to go to the bathroom." I raised a brow, my fight or flight reaction kicking in. As usual, I chose the hard way.

"How long have you been waiting?" He glanced down at his watch. "*Merda*. I'm sorry I am so late." The downturn of his lips led me to believe that he was actually repentant. "My business meeting ran behind."

I couldn't help the fake chuckle that escaped my lips. "Sure it did."

Sal spoke from behind me in Italian, and then he and Marco exchanged a few sentences. When Marco's gaze flickered down to me again, I thought I saw a flash of concern but his words indicated otherwise. "Come. Let's go. I'm playing poker tonight, and I want you with me."

I knew better than to mention Alexa. I had no right. And it could very well mean the end of my time with Marco—and more importantly, the money he was providing. So I drew a deep breath and stuffed down my irritation until I almost choked on it, ready to get on with the evening.

"There you are." I turned to see Leroy heading toward us, a crease between his eyebrows. "I was wondering what the hell happened when you didn't come back."

"Sorry, something caught my eye on the way and I got sidetracked," I responded with a brief glance at Marco. His eyes darkened.

"Let us be going now," Marco said. Gripping my

upper arm a little roughly, he began to lead me away.

"Easy there." Leroy put a hand on Marco's shoulder, dipping his head and clearly issuing a warning without words.

Sal took a step forward. Marco's lips snarled and he looked down at Leroy's hand on his light gray suit jacket.

The tension in the air had ratcheted up to F5 tornado level, the air heavy in my lungs as I breathed it in.

My gaze bounced around the three of them, wondering which would be the one to break the silence first.

Seemed that would be me.

"Alright, boys. Play nice." I patted Leroy on the chest to try and get his attention, noticing when I turned back to look at Marco how his narrowed eyes were fixed on my hand.

"'Kay girl, you get going. I won't be far behind." Leroy dropped his hand from Marco's shoulder and he took a step back.

I exhaled a relieved breath as the strain dissipated from Marco's features and his attention returned to me. A smile ghosted across his face, and he let go of my arm and then held his own out for me to take of my own accord. "Shall we?"

I returned his smile in an attempt to put the discomfort of the past few minutes behind us.

"Certainly." I wound my arm through his, and then he led us toward the high-stakes poker area after giving some directive to Sal in Italian.

We were silent for a beat when Marco finally spoke. "That meatman cares for you." A giggle escaped my lips, and he turned his head and looked down at me. "Why do you laugh?"

"The word isn't—" Another giggle escaped and I fought for control. "It's not meatman, it's meathead."

I'm not sure why, but I couldn't seem to get a hold of myself. Marco stopped us and gazed down at me, observing intently as I continued to laugh harder and harder, more likely than not looking like I was either a crazy person or on some type of recreational drug.

To my surprise, he wasn't angry that I was basically mocking him. Instead, my laughter caught in my throat as I took in the hunger in his eyes.

"You are very beautiful when you laugh," he said, cupping my cheek with his hand.

"Thank you," I said softly, not even sure if he could hear me over all the noise in the casino.

"You should do it more often."

Before I could respond, he'd linked our arms together and we were once again making our way to our destination.

"So, you enjoy poker?" I asked, now that I'd gotten a hold of myself.

"On occasion. Though I don't normally like throwing my money away with no assurance that I'll be getting anything back for it."

"We're in agreement there. I've been in Vegas many years now, and I can count on one hand the number of times I've gambled."

We'd reached Bobby's Room, but instead of directing us inside, Marco pulled us to a stop just outside the door.

"Did you grow up here?" He seemed genuinely interested in my answer. Part of me wanted to open up to him, even though it wasn't something I ever did with a client. I was beginning to realize that I might actually long for that kind of connection with another person—the ability to talk freely about yourself.

"No, I grew up in Utah," I said before my thoughts

could run away from me any further.

He brushed the hair on one side of my head behind my ear. "That is good. I cannot imagine raising a child amongst all this," he said, gesturing around him.

That stung. "There are plenty of children raised here, Marco. There's more to Las Vegas than just the strip."

My voice held too much ire, and Marco had definitely picked up on it. His head tilted to the side as he regarded me. "Perhaps you will show me this one day."

I pressed my full lips together and gave him a curt nod. *Not likely.*

"Good. Now let's get me checked in so that I may donate my money to the casino."

Marco spoke to the hostess, and a few minutes later we were seated at one of the poker tables. Drinks were served as the dealer shuffled the cards, preparing to start the game.

I was the only female at the table, and most of the men appeared to be a decade or two older than Marco. We were seated opposite the only man who didn't appear to belong with this crowd. While most of the people in the room displayed their wealth with pride, for all intents and purposes, he appeared pretty...regular. The man could've used a hair cut a couple of weeks ago, he wore no jewelry, and though he wore a collared shirt, it looked like it'd come off a rack at Target rather than a designer boutique. I knew for a fact that not everyone who was wealthy in this town showcased it for all to see, so I pushed the thought from my head.

I sat silently as a few hands were dealt, quietly observing. I found it appalling how these men threw away their money as if it meant nothing. There was so much good that could be done with the chips sitting on this table.

Marco won his third hand in a row, and he grinned as he raked the chips toward him. When he was finished arranging them, he regarded me with a warm smile. "Perhaps you are my good luck charm."

I laughed, pretty certain that wasn't the case. Nothing had ever happened in my life that would make anyone think I could be considered lucky. Quite the opposite, in fact. My last name should've been Murphy.

The gentleman across from us spoke up when I was done laughing. "Seen uglier good luck charms in my day," he said with a Southern drawl and winked at me. "Hell, one of my buddies used to wear the same underwear every time we hit the casino because he won big in them one night. Never even washed 'em."

Marco shook his head. "I'll take Brandi here over that any day."

"Can't say as I blame you." The man picked up the glass in front of him and took a healthy sip. "Gus Albright's my name. Pleasure to meet you, Brandi and..."

"Marco. Marco Valenti." He nodded in Gus's direction.

The two of them chatted for a bit while playing cards, with me interjecting every once and awhile. Something clicked for me when Gus answered one of Marco's seemingly innocent questions.

"Do you live in Vegas, Gus?" Marco asked.

The older man nodded. "Yeah, work for the city now. I'm a City Council member." *Interesting*, I thought, but didn't dare say so. "I'm guessing from the accent that you're not from here?"

"You're a smart man, Gus. No, I'm from Italy. I'm in town to see about securing the property on Canyon Avenue for development. You know the one?"

Gus nodded slowly this time, like he was assessing Marco, sizing him up. "Lots of interest in that property."

"So I heard. I spoke with Alexa Sands today. Maybe I have a fight on my hands to get it?"

I shifted in my seat, hating myself a little for the way that her name uttered on his lips made me want to punch someone.

Gus peered across the table from under his brows as the dealer distributed cards for the next hand. "Alexa, you say?"

"Sí."

Gus didn't respond, only pursed his lips and nodded as if he were taking in exactly what this all meant.

The next few rounds were played in silence. I sat patiently like the eye candy I was meant to be and sipped on my drink. Marco's phone vibrated from inside his suit jacket, and he pulled it out to take a look. I wasn't able to see what the text message on his screen said, but as I discreetly took another sip of my drink, I definitely saw his response. *It's done.*

I was busy trying to figure out what the hell that meant when Marco rested his hand on the bare skin above my knee. He trailed a path up my thigh inch by inch, and the urge to squirm in my seat was so intense I had to dig my fingernails into my palms as a way to distract myself from it.

I glanced around the table. No one else seemed to notice. They were far too into the game and their attempts to win the large amount of chips in the center of the table.

The closer he got to the juncture of my thighs, the shallower my breathing became. Not wanting to come undone in front of a room full of people, I squeezed my thighs together. Marco gave me a cutting side-eye that pretty much told me what he thought of that, and I relaxed my legs once again. But he didn't remove his hand.

When he was close to his destination, he extended one finger and brushed lightly over the silk of my panties. I bit my lip to prevent myself from crying out.

A chorus of yells and cursing burst out of the men sitting around the table, tearing us both from the moment.

Marco removed his hand and straightened up in his chair. I crossed my legs, both relieved and disappointed by the interruption.

A few more rounds of cards went by, the men at the table chatting amiably, when Sal appeared at Marco's side, his arms crossed in front of him and his mouth in a straight line. Bending down, Sal whispered something to Marco, whose hand shot out and gripped my leg while his gazed darted all around us.

I had no idea what was going on, but it was clear that the easygoing persona Marco had projected earlier had vanished, and in its place was a man that was as frightening as he was fierce.

CHAPTER FOURTEEN

Marco stood abruptly from his chair. "Gentleman, it appears I have business I must attend to. I wish you all luck." He smiled, but it didn't reach his eyes.

Sal collected the chips while Marco moved behind me and slid my chair out. I thanked him, grabbed my purse, and stood to join him.

He wrapped his arm around me, resting it on my lower back. It was scary how much I was beginning to find comfort in his arms.

Just as we turned to make our exit, Gus's voice rang out from behind us. "Hold up there, Mr. Valenti."

Marco swung us around to face the man who was now walking around the table in our direction under the watchful eye of Sal.

"If you don't find Alexa helpful enough, be sure to give me a call." Gus's hand slid in his pocket and emerged with a white business card.

Marco nodded, gave his thanks, and then we were out of there. He led us quickly across the multi-colored carpet of the casino, beyond rows and rows of noisy slot machines.

"Where's the fire?" I asked. It was difficult to keep up in my four-inch platform heels.

He didn't slow down, but he did turn his head to look at me. "What does this mean?" he asked in a clipped tone.

"It's an expression. It means, why are we in such a hurry?"

Marco's hand on my lower back tensed for a heartbeat. "I'm anxious to get you back to my suite." His hand slid down from my back to my ass and he squeezed. "Is that so hard to believe?"

A small part of me thrilled—a small, girly part of me. And I hated that part of me at the moment, because she had no business getting excited about comments like that.

Besides, I didn't believe him. Oh, I knew I could get the man excited; the blowjob in his suite a few days ago proved that. But Marco consistently put his business before pleasure, and the one conclusion I'd drawn at the poker table that evening was that he was most definitely there on business.

So the question remained—why did we have to leave so abruptly?

"Brandi?"

"Sorry." I shook my head, pushing my suspicions to the back of my mind. It wasn't my place to know anyway. "Of course not. I'm looking forward to returning to your suite as well."

We reached the elevator in silence, and Sal pressed the button then turned to scan the area behind us. By the time the elevator dinged, a host of other people were waiting with us. Leroy wasn't one of them, though I had no doubt he was somewhere close by.

Marco kept me tucked close to his side on the ride up. I couldn't help but breathe in his scent, and it sent flutters through my stomach.

We were the last ones to exit the car, and even though Sal had stepped off with us, he didn't follow. Instead, he stayed off to the side of the elevators, watching our retreat.

As soon as we entered the suite, Marco retreated to the master and I settled on the sofa to await his instructions, quickly checking my phone for any messages from Martina. Nothing from her, but Vivian had called again. God, she was relentless in trying to get me to leave Sylvia. I deleted her message without listening to it.

Marco returned a few minutes later wearing a pair of lounge pants and a tight gray t-shirt that displayed the abundance of muscles underneath it.

"So you do wear something other than a suit," I observed good-naturedly.

That earned me a small laugh that was well worth the risk of possibly upsetting him.

"On occasion."

He walked behind the bar, where he removed the cork from a bottle of red wine, poured us each a glass, and then returned to sit beside me on the sofa. He held out one of the wine glasses and I took it from him, my fingers brushing against his when I did.

His gaze caught mine, and it was so full of want—of *need*—that I inhaled shakily.

I raised the glass to my mouth and took a sip of the dark liquid. "Mmm. That's really nice wine."

"Nothing but the best *for* the best." His eyes remained locked on me, causing me to blush.

I attempted to change the subject. "You were doing

quite well earlier. Why the sudden departure? I figured we might be there for a while."

Marco paused with his glass halfway to his mouth and shrugged. "I had my reasons." He took a sip of his wine and set the glass on the table.

This man and his non-answers were going to make me crazy. It was obvious he wasn't in a sharing mood, and normally I'd have let it drop, but I was getting tired of the mysterious Marco. I wanted *some* answers.

"Is it a coincidence that at every event we've been to there's someone there from the city who has something to do with land development?"

Marco's eyes acted like a camera shutter, widening before narrowing to take me in. I almost broke down and changed the subject. Almost. But no, I would match his gaze until he gave me *something*.

I didn't like not being in control, and with Marco, everything—especially my feelings—felt out of control.

"Well?" I prodded.

"What do you think?" He arched an eyebrow.

I took his response as verification that I was indeed correct. And although Marco could have been using these opportunities to meet the right people in order to successfully bid for the city property, my gut told me it was something else.

"I think there's more to it."

"Careful how far out you wade," he said in a low voice laced with warning. "These are shark-infested waters."

"I'm pretty good at staying in the shallow end."

Marco reached out and wrapped his large hand around the front of my neck, his thumb grazing along my rapidly heating skin ever so slowly.

"That's where most sharks prefer to do their hunting...where their victims least expect it."

I drew in a deep, shaky breath and his hand tightened just a fraction around the column of my neck. *God, why was this such a turn-on?*

"So you're saying I'm wrong?" I asked softly.

"I'm saying I'm not paying you to ask questions," he said, still holding my neck.

At the mention of my fee, my eyes widened. I'd completely forgotten to get my money at the beginning of the night. That had never happened before. Ever. We may have had an agreement that he'd pay me every night regardless of whether he used my services or not, but I still had to collect the money owed to me since the last time I'd seen him.

I'd been so blinded by jealousy after witnessing Marco and Alexa together, the thought hadn't even crossed my mind. As if I'd been on a real date with this man.

Damn it. I was so screwed.

Not only had it slipped my mind that we were conducting business here, but thinking of Alexa again made a sick, bitter sensation rise up from my stomach.

"What is it you're thinking, cara?" Marco continued to swipe his thumb along my neck, and I hated that I was acutely aware of everywhere this man made contact with me.

I wasn't able to stop myself before the words flew past my lips. "What about Alexa?" I asked, her name dripping with venom when it left my mouth.

His thumb stopped moving, and he pinned me with a stare that suggested both irritation and interest. *God, why couldn't I keep my mouth shut?*

"What about her?"

"I saw you two earlier," I admitted in a small voice.

He tensed. It was only a small amount, but I noticed.

"We were discussing business."

"Seemed like she was interested in more than business to me."

"She was." I pulled back, surprised at his honesty. His hand dropped to his side. "Does that mean I am interested in her?"

"You tell me." I wanted to gouge my own eyes out at this point. I sounded like a petulant child.

"Have you not realized that there is only *one* woman who has captivated me since the moment I met her? *One* woman who I cannot seem to pry from my thoughts. *One* woman who I want to please." He punctuated his last statement by putting his hand on my breast and thumbing my nipple through the fabric.

My breath caught and my heart stuttered over its next beat before I was able to respond. "I...I didn't know that, no."

Marco leaned in, his delicious scent wafting my way as he did, and brought his lips to the column of my neck. A small shiver stole down my body and headed directly to the apex of my thighs.

"Now you do. I'm done discussing this. Suffice it to say I will use Alexa for business as I see fit, and that's all you need to know."

Marco's warm tongue trailed a path up to my earlobe, where he gently bit down. A small whimper left my mouth and he groaned. Then he continued to kiss and lick and suck on my neck, so I wrapped my arms around him, pushing one hand into his hair and splaying the other one on his back. The feel of his muscles as they flexed and relaxed while his hands explored my body was almost too much for me. I wanted to strip this man bare and explore *his* body.

Thoughts of Alexa drifted away as Marco's hands cupped my ass, pressing me firmly against him. His nose trailed a path along the edge of my jaw until he reached my ear.

"Tell me your real name," he said in a low, ragged voice. I stilled for the briefest of seconds, but it was enough for Marco to know he was onto something. "Tell me."

"You already know my name."

One of his hands slid to my hip and down to the seam of my dress, which he pulled up slowly. Then he dipped his hand between my legs.

"Do you think me an idiot? Brandi is not your real name." He slid my lace underwear to the side, and then slid his fingers through my wetness and over my clit, causing a whimper to escape.

"That *is* my name." His fingers coasted over my clit again and my hands shot up to grip his shoulders for support.

"I will leave it for now, bella. Only because I cannot wait any longer to be inside you."

"Thank you," I whispered, grinding against his fingers.

"But you *will* tell me. Let it be when you trust me completely."

I would never allow myself to trust him with all of me, but I didn't share that with Marco. Instead, I ran a hand down his chest until I felt the hard outline of his cock underneath his pants. I squeezed him and Marco pulled my hand away.

"Not here. I want to take my time with you, and I don't want to worry about interruptions." Intertwining our fingers, he led me into the bedroom.

The first thing I noticed was that it was as tidy as the rest of the suite. Nothing was out of place and there were no clothes lying around on top of the rich mahogany furniture or the plush beige carpet.

Looking to gain any information I could on the man who was making this place home, I dropped Marco's hand and walked over to the dresser, dragging my hand along the wood while I examined the contents. There wasn't much there. His watch, wallet, a book in Italian—it appeared to be business related—and a money clip filled with neatly organized bills. The various items were all meticulously aligned with an equal amount of distance between each.

"What are you doing?" I glanced over to Marco, who leaned in the doorway with his arms crossed over his chest, an amused expression on his face.

"Trying to learn a little more about you." Thankfully, he chuckled at my boldness and wasn't offended.

I returned my attention to the dresser and picked up the book, thumbing through it for a moment before putting it back down. Then I continued to the other side of the room to see if there was anything interesting there.

"This is a nice room, but it barely looks lived in."

"I like things orderly." Out of the corner of my eye, I saw Marco head over to where I'd just been standing and correct the placement of the book.

That was when it struck me. Marco was a clean freak...or a control freak...or both. A soft giggle escaped me and his gaze darted across the room.

"Something amusing?" He arched an eyebrow, but one corner of his mouth rose so I knew he wasn't angry.

"You. You're a neat freak. That's why this entire suite barely looks lived in every time I'm here."

The thought of this powerful man, who seemed to let nothing faze him, allowing something as small as the placement of a book to get under his skin seemed comical to me.

He smirked. "You find it funny?"

"You're not denying it?" I laughed again.

"I like things in their place. There is nothing wrong with that." He stepped away from the dresser and began walking toward me. I backed up a few paces, feeling playful.

"You like control," I taunted.

"Perhaps," he said. "Or maybe I just like everything in its place, like I said."

"And where would you like to place *me* right now?"

His eyelids dipped, and he took a quick look at the bed then back at me. "I think you know exactly where I want you."

"Well, maybe you should position me there exactly how you want me." I issued the challenge while stepping back, so I was on the opposite side of the bed as Marco.

Without warning, he dashed to the end of the bed, trying to make his way around to my side. Laughing, I dove across the bed and scrambled until I'd made it to the other side, out of his reach.

Marco regarded me and bit down on his lip. "You don't understand how much I like the chase, tesoro. This is simply foreplay to me."

His words must have had a direct line to my clit because the damn thing was throbbing and begging for attention. It was all I could do not to plop myself down on the mattress and beg Marco to take me. Either that or put my own hand between my thighs.

I wouldn't be letting him know that though. "Well,

let's see if you can keep up," I taunted.

Marco ran around the end of the bed, leaving me no choice but to crawl back over the top of it to escape him. I was on my hands and knees on the far side of the bed, almost in the clear, when his hand clamped around my ankle and dragged me back toward him.

I yelped and scrambled for purchase on the mattress as I slid along, managing only to pull apart the bed, which, of course, had been neatly made.

My legs were now dangling off the end of the bed and my dress bunched up to my waist, exposing my black garters and lace underwear. Marco's body covered mine now, the weight of him pressing my stomach into the mattress.

"Te l'avevo detto che non mi saresti sfuggita." He pushed his hips forward. "I told you that you could not escape."

"Maybe I wasn't trying to." I pushed my ass up into him and felt his hard length through his pants. Heat pooled between my thighs as I imagined him pulling down his pants, pushing my scrap of underwear to the side, and taking me right then and there.

"Were you merely teasing me, cara?" His hand traced a path from the side of my knee up my thigh to my hip bone. I closed my eyes and imagined that we were a real couple, just back from dinner, about to enjoy the pleasure one another's bodies could bring.

It was almost comical how easily you could fool yourself when you really wanted to.

Marco's breathing picked up and he leaned down further to place a kiss on my shoulder. His body slid over mine, creating a delicious friction. Then he slid down so his knees rested on the carpet below, his face level with my core.

"Marco," I whispered, both on fire and uncomfortable at his intimate appraisal.

I tried to shift up the mattress, but Marco's hands at my waist stilled me. He slid them down over my ass and massaged. "Sei perfetta, mia cara."

"In English?" I managed to ask.

"I was commenting on how perfect you are." He leaned forward and traced a path with his tongue up the globe of my ass. "You're all I think about."

My already shallow breathing hitched. "Really?"

Marco drew my black thong down slowly as far as it would go before my garters got in the way. My heart raced in my chest, pounding against the inside of my ribcage as I anticipated what he'd do next.

"This is so hard to believe?" He ran his lips over one cheek, delivering chaste kisses then running his tongue along before biting into my flesh. It felt like he was touching me everywhere but where I really wanted to feel him.

I squirmed, silently begging for him to dip into the wetness I knew must be visible between my legs. Fisting the comforter in my hands, I pressed my forehead into the mattress, attempting in vain to quell my impatience. "Marco, please," I begged.

"Mmm," he moaned. "I think I like the sound of you begging."

He finally ran a finger along the length of me, spreading my wetness back and forth, but without enough pressure to breach me. He was careful to avoid my clit, the bastard.

I tried moving my hips and forcing him where I wanted him, but to no avail. Desperation bloomed in my chest and my single-minded focus was to get Marco inside me.

"Well?" he asked. I was so worked up that I wasn't able to make sense of his question.

"What?" I moaned, shifting my hips around, hoping to somehow force him to do my bidding. I needn't have bothered. It was clear that Marco did things in his own time.

"Why does it surprise you that I think of you when we are not together?"

More swirling. More denying me.

"You could have any woman," I said between gritted teeth while I fisted the comforter. "Why would you think of me? I'm an escort."

I heard the rustle of fabric, and I imagined that he was pulling his pants down. I hoped anyway.

He stood and leaned down over me, the scent of his expensive cologne enveloping me. I drew in a deep breath to savor it.

Marco brushed the head of his cock through the wetness of my pussy, and I moaned. Never had I been closer to begging a man to take me.

Then he brought his lips to my ear and spoke in a low voice. "That is what you do, mia cara. It's clear to anyone who meets you that it is not *who* you are."

I didn't know what to say, and it didn't matter. A second later Marco pushed himself into me, and I was breathless at the feel of him stretching and filling me.

His large hands wrapped around my waist. "Do you know how many times I imagined what it would feel like once I finally got inside you? How many times I fisted my own cock pretending it was your heat wrapped around me?"

I pushed my face into the mattress and moaned, his words only stoking the blazing inferno inside me.

He thrust in and out of my slick heat, dragging his thick cock back until he'd almost left me, then slamming back in with a satisfied grunt.

"I knew you'd feel this good, tesoro. Your pussy is perfection."

His hands explored my ass cheeks, massaging them and pulling them apart to expose all of me for his viewing. Marco pumped in and out of me while his thumb spread my wetness over my puckered hole. He played with me, circling the rim with his thumb.

"One day soon I will have this ass."

Yes, I wanted to shout, because in that moment I would've done or said whatever he told me to. Hell, I would've been happy to hand over my soul to the man on a silver-rimmed platter if he'd just keep doing what he was doing to my body.

He shifted his hips so he drove into me at an angle that was more intense.

"Marco!" I cried out, gripping the sheets even tighter and pushing back to meet his thrusts.

He gripped the back of my hair and pulled my head so I was able to see him in my peripheral vision.

"I want to know something." He was breathing harder and his voice was strained. Then he continued without waiting for a response from me. "Do you think of me when we are not together?"

He punctuated his last word with a brutal thrust forward that had me crying out.

"Why...why would you ask that?" I somehow managed to respond. My entire body felt as if it were embroiled in an inferno.

"Tell me. Do you think of me?" The hand holding my

hair squeezed tighter and my head pulled back even farther so that I met his gaze. He didn't even blink as he continued to pound into me.

His dark eyes never gave much away, but I saw desire there—only this time it was desire for more than just my body. It was for the truth. And so, for the first time I could remember, I allowed the truth to tumble from my lips in front of a client.

"All the time." I broke eye contact with him and he let my head fall to the mattress. Admitting the truth to him somehow made me feel weak.

"Brava, cosi'si fa." I had no idea what he'd said, but the satisfaction in his voice was clear.

Marco reached a hand around and spread my wetness over my clit in a way that had every nerve ending in my body tingling and tightening until I finally detonated.

Both of Marco's hands went to my waist as I cried out and jerked back against him. My vision swam and I squeezed my eyes shut, exulting in the first orgasm I'd had courtesy of a man—ever.

I was aware of Marco's own harsh cry from behind me, the feel of his sweaty chest pressed against my back, and the weight of him pressing me into the bed, but not much more than that.

As I clenched around him, I was no longer a woman with a life and hopes and dreams. I was simply a vessel, filled to the brim and overflowing with pleasure. There was no beginning and no end. No right and wrong. No client and provider.

When I came back to myself, Marco was still inside me. He swept my hair to one side then leaned down further and placed a kiss on my shoulder.

"I knew we would be amazing together."
I didn't admit it to him, but I'd known it, too.

CHAPTER FIFTEEN

An hour later Marco had ordered gelato up to the room and we remained in his bed, enjoying the cold treat while *Two Broke Girls* played on the television. He'd let me choose.

Naked, with the sheet pulled up to his waist, Marco was the most relaxed I'd ever seen him. Gone was the almost perma-crease between his brows as he leaned against the headboard, savoring his dessert.

It seemed orgasms agreed with him.

He laughed wholeheartedly at something Max had said on the show, and I gazed at him in curiosity and awe. It was odd seeing him like this—odd but welcome—and I knew when he glanced over at me with the warmth still radiating from his eyes that I was a goner.

"Why do you hire women for sex?" I blurted it out before I could help myself. It'd been on my mind, and I wanted to know all there was to know about Marco. I was woman enough to admit to myself that I wanted something I had a feeling no other woman ever had—I wanted to know the *real* him.

"What makes you think you are not the first?"

I shrugged. "It's a guess. But you can usually tell when it's a man's first time." I brought my spoon to my mouth and sucked the strawberry-flavored treat from the cold metal. Marco's gaze darted to my lips and his lids grew heavy.

"Oh?"

"They're nervous and unsure what to do...they don't know when the exchange of money normally happens...they're shocked to find Leroy with me. You were none of those things."

"And what was I?" he asked, setting his bowl and spoon on the bedside table. Then he immediately repositioned the spoon in the bowl so that it was his version of perfect.

I decided to be honest with him. "A man in control who knew what he wanted. Even if that wasn't getting me naked the first couple of times." I returned my gaze to the television, embarrassed that I'd let him know how much it had bothered me.

The bowl and spoon were plucked from my hands. I glanced over at Marco and watched as he positioned them on his bedside table along with his own.

He turned his attention back to me then reached out to grip my hand. "I was hard within seconds after opening my door to you. Make no mistake, I wanted you...then and there, and every moment since."

Every girly part of me rejoiced inside.

I immediately wanted to smother every single one of those parts, because I should *not* care.

"Why did you blow me off then?" I couldn't help but ask.

"If memory serves, you were the one blowing me."

He grinned.

I smacked his chest. "I'm serious."

He blew out a breath and leaned back against the headboard. "I had to attend to something that could not wait. Believe me, if I had any choice in the matter, I would have spent the evening with you coming apart around my cock. But the choice wasn't mine."

"I see." I shifted at the memory of exactly how exquisite that had felt.

"To answer your first question about why I hire escorts, it's pretty simple. I'm a busy man. I know what I like, and though I'm not averse to relationships, my schedule makes it difficult to maintain one. I have needs and I have money. I see no reason why a business arrangement with a willing female shouldn't satisfy those needs."

"Gotcha. It's business." My voice was strained, though I had tried to keep the edge out of it.

I couldn't fault him for his logic. Everything he said was true, and really, I subscribed to the same theory. My hooking was business and nothing more.

I tried not to think of Marco with other women—other women he paid to sleep with him—but images assaulted my thoughts anyway, and the little green monster that had taken hold of me earlier transformed into one worthy of Hulk status.

I sat leaning against the headboard with my arms crossed, staring straight ahead at the TV. The show continued, but I heard none of it until Marco's voice cut through the din.

"Are you upset?" he asked. I detected a note of surprise in his voice.

"Of course not." I inhaled a deep breath in an

attempt to relax my muscles, and it worked...sort of.

Before I even knew what happened, Marco had me pinned beneath him with my hands above my head, a wide grin spread across his face.

"What are you doing?" I bucked my hips in an effort to dislodge him.

"You are angry that I used the word 'business.'" That stupid grin was still on Marco's face.

"I. Am. Not." Mostly I was just mad at myself for falling into the trap that had been the undoing of many a working girl before me—falling for your client.

I tried pulling my hands free, but it was no use.

"Get off me, Marco," I grumbled.

He didn't listen to me. What he did do was grow hard against my stomach as he leaned over the top of me, and I was forced to look up at the perfect male specimen while I lay naked underneath him.

My insides grew hot and my nipples tightened of their own accord. *Damn my treacherous body.*

Marco smirked at me from above. "It bothers you to think of me with other women. And you were jealous of Alexa. At first, I thought maybe you were afraid she would replace you in my bed and I would no longer need your services." He gave a short laugh. Seeing him this way was almost worth ignoring the fact that it was at my expense. "Now I see it is jealousy."

I rolled my eyes. "Pfft. Please. Why should it matter to me who you choose to sleep with?"

He leaned down and nuzzled my neck with his nose, dragging it lightly along my hairline, across my jaw, and finally over my cheek before he leaned in next to my ear and whispered, "For the same reason it matters to me who you fuck."

I sucked in a breath, not sure what to make of his comment. Marco released my hands and stretched himself out over me, using his knees to spread my legs. He looked down at me with dark, fathomless eyes filled with possession, causing a shiver to wrack my entire body.

"Rest assured, tesoro. We are definitely *not* just business."

Before I could respond, he sunk himself into me with a groan, and being the coward I was, I decided to lose myself in him physically rather than examine how I was losing my heart.

CHAPTER SIXTEEN

"You always seem so fascinated with those," Marco said as I gazed out the window to the fountain show below.

I smiled and looked back over my shoulder at him. "It's hard not to be, don't you think?"

So far we'd spent a lovely evening relaxing inside Marco's suite, and as usual I'd gravitated over to the window to gaze down at the illustrious display below.

Marco moved closer and placed his hands on each of my shoulders, giving them a squeeze. "I was distracted by the beauty of something else, so I can't really say."

I rolled my eyes and smiled. "Always such a charmer."

Marco dipped his head and kissed the area where my neck met my shoulder. I closed my eyes briefly to enjoy the sensation of his lips on my skin.

"So I *can* divert your attention from the fountains." I laughed. "Have you ever watched the show from the street?"

I turned in his arms to face him. "No. Have you?"

He shook his head. "Why don't we go down and watch? Enjoy it as it was meant to be enjoyed."

"Really?"

He met my enthusiasm with an amused grin. "Really."

I pushed up on my tiptoes and gave him a chaste kiss. "Let's go!"

I practically dragged him out of the suite, and once we reached the hallway where Sal was stationed, Marco let him know what we were up to. Sal didn't look pleased for some reason and tried to talk us out of going down to the strip to watch, but Marco took one look at the excitement on my face and told him it was happening.

The three of us took the elevator down, and exiting the casino, we followed the path along the edge of the manmade lake, which was situated at the front of the hotel on the strip. A show had just ended a minute before, so the crowd was busy coming and going. I felt a little like a salmon swimming upstream as we made our way through the throngs of people.

Marco held firmly onto my hand and eventually we made it to the sidewalk on the strip.

"Where would you like to stand?" Marco asked me.

"Can we get as close as possible to the middle of the lake?" I figured that would be the best vantage point.

"Of course." Marco turned and continued to lead the way through the crowd, and I held tight to his hand.

A couple of minutes later we were closer to our destination and he directed us out of the mass of people on the sidewalk and closer to the railing along the edge of the lake.

"We're pretty close to the middle now. I'm going to

try to find us a spot right up against the railing."

A minute later Marco had snuck us into one of the few remaining positions at the railing. He positioned himself behind me with his arms wrapped around my waist, and we waited.

I looked at the still black water of the small lake, excited for what was to come. I'd been on the strip many times, of course, but I'd never seen the show from here or experienced it the way a tourist did. Normally, I saw it while driving by on my way to meet a client.

The murmurs of the crowd became louder, and everyone seemed to grow restless waiting for the next performance to start. The shows were every fifteen minutes this time of night, so it shouldn't be long.

"I wonder what song it's going to be." I tilted my head back to look at Marco, who was smiling down at me.

Before he could answer, the first notes of a musical score boomed out of the speakers, and I whipped my head back around so I didn't miss a thing.

The crowd grew quiet as the first line of fountains lit up and the water began to dance. After a few seconds went by, I realized that I recognized the song.

Marco leaned down and said into my ear, "'Con Te Partiro' by Andrea Bocelli."

I was about to open my mouth to argue with him when the rich voice began singing, and sure enough it was in Italian. I wasn't familiar with this version, but the English equivalent was "Time To Say Goodbye."

We watched as the fountains danced in synchronization to the music, sometimes making long sweeping motions from one side to the next and at other times bursting high in the air.

The feeling of being held in Marco's arms, the exquisite song, and the beauty of the fountain show caused tears to form in the corners of my eyes. As Bocelli held the last long note and the fountains shot straight up toward the sky, one lone tear escaped and ran down my cheek. I wasn't happy nor was I sad, just bursting full of emotion that needed an outlet to escape.

The last of the music faded away and the lights illuminating the lake turned off, leaving us to once again stare at the still, black water. The crowd surrounding the fountain cheered.

I quickly swiped away my tear before turning back to Marco. "That was amazing. Thank you for suggesting we come down here to see it."

He bent quickly to kiss me. "Do you want to stay for the next one?"

I shook my head. The perfection of the moment had left me so content that I didn't want to steal from it by hanging around to watch another song.

"Let's head back to the room then." His eyes had that glint about them, and I knew what he had in mind. I was all for it.

I nodded and then Marco cast a glance over my head—to find Sal, I presumed. He lifted his chin before taking my hand and leading me back the way we came.

The large sidewalk in front of the strip seemed even more packed now. It was slow going, and not being as tall as Marco, I couldn't see much of anything except for his back.

Eventually, he led us closer to the edge of the sidewalk where it met the road. The crowd was a little thinner here and we were able to move a little easier.

We made steady progress until we were forced to

walk around a crowd of people who had stopped to watch some kid perform break-dancing moves. Everyone not interested in watching tried to squeeze back to the middle of the sidewalk to get around them.

Somewhere along the way I was jostled, and my hand slipped from Marco's. Before I could grab it again, he was swallowed up by the crowd. I kept moving forward, figuring I'd spot him at some point. I couldn't have stopped if I wanted to—not without being trampled anyway.

I thought I saw him frantically looking around for me a little ways ahead, and I began making my way in that direction. I tried by best, but the momentum of the crowd kept pushing me closer and closer to the road.

Damn it.

The next thing I knew someone shoved me hard from behind, and I went flying out toward the road. I stumbled on the curb and landed on the pavement, and before I had a second to register my predicament, the sound of screeching brakes assaulted my ears and bright headlights filled my vision.

I screamed and threw my arms up in a futile attempt to shield myself just as the car came to a stop a few inches in front of me. I was aware of some commotion on the sidewalk, and a moment later both Marco and Sal appeared in front of me.

"What the hell happened?" Marco asked as the two of them helped me to stand.

My heart beat so hard that I could barely make out his words over the thumping sound in my ears. I was trembling as I attempted to stand on my own. Marco wrapped his arms around me and drew me into his chest. "Are you okay?"

I nodded, jerky movements to accompany the full

body shake I had going on.

"She's in shock," I heard Sal say from behind me.

Before I knew what was happening, Marco had me in his arms and was walking quickly back to the hotel. The crowd seemed to realize something was going on and miraculously made room for us to pass.

When I found my voice again, I spoke. "It felt like someone pushed me from behind. I don't know if they tripped or were just fooling around or what. One minute I was making my way through all the people, and the next I was sprawled out on the road."

Marco squeezed me a bit tighter and I looked up at his face. He swept a sidelong glance over at Sal, and something passed between them.

He bent down to kiss the top of my head. "Don't worry. I'm going to take care of you."

Right before we entered the lobby of the hotel, a Celine Dion song started playing from the fountain area, marking the beginning of the next show.

I was still shaken, but I'd be fine. Wrong place, wrong time.

"I can walk now," I said as we approached the elevators.

"Are you sure?" Marco's brows were drawn like he didn't believe me, but I nodded so he gently set me down.

"Thank you," I said.

Sal pressed the button to call the elevator.

"No thanks necessary," he said, leaning in again to kiss the top of my head. "I meant what I said. I *will* take care of you."

Marco was a man of his word. After the multiple orgasms he gave me later that night, I'd never felt more taken care of.

CHAPTER SEVENTEEN

Weeks went by with the same routine—I spent my days loving my son and my nights lusting after Marco. We no longer discussed payment since I saw him every night. Instead, he'd leave an envelope for me on the table by the suite door, which I'd slip into my purse without comment on the way out.

We'd just finished a delicious dinner in his suite, but I was unable to stop the niggling feeling that something was off. Sure, he'd seemed more introspective and quiet than usual, but I figured it could have been business related.

Marco led me to the living area and sat me down on the couch, though he remained standing in front of me. Looking down at me with a drawn face, he said, "I have another proposition for you."

"I'm listening..." Though I'd liked his first proposition, something about the way he'd said it had my blood running sluggishly through my veins.

"What if I told you that you had to move in here with me?" His tone was grim.

What the hell was he talking about? I cocked my head. "Why would I *have* to move in with you?"

For the first time since we'd met, Marco was visibly shaken. It was unsettling as hell. He'd always been so calm and in control, even when I could tell he wasn't happy about something. Without responding, he began pacing across the room.

"Some people—*bad* people—have taken notice of you."

My blood now slowed to a glacial pace as ice crept into my veins. "Okay...so they've noticed me. What exactly does that mean?"

He spun on his heel and pinned me with a penetrating stare. "These are people you don't want to fuck with, tesoro."

I crossed my arms over my chest. "The only person I've *fucked*, Marco, is you."

He was in front of me in three long and powerful strides, looking down at me with narrowed eyes. "And that's how it will remain."

We stayed like that for a minute, neither of us willing to break the connection first. Finally, in the interest of putting an end to this conversation, I shattered the silence. "I'm not moving in with you."

"You will."

"I most certainly will not." I stood and poked a finger at his chest as my ire grew. "You may pay for my evenings, but you don't *own* me. No one does. Believe it or not, I have my own life and it doesn't involve being on my back twenty-four-seven."

Marco cradled my face in his hands. Though the look

on his face was severe, his touch was soft, almost reverent. "I would *never* want to own you."

I closed my eyes and tried to quell my rising emotions. Marco's thumb grazed my cheek ever so softly, and I leaned into his touch. "I can't move in with you," I whispered.

"You will."

I opened my eyes to look into his dark ones, willing him to see what I couldn't tell him. "You don't understand...I *can't.*"

"Your life is in danger."

I froze. Every muscle in my body contracted, and I stopped breathing for a moment as his words set in. "What do you mean my life is in danger? That's not the same as someone noticing me." Panic had crept into my voice, and I inhaled deeply to dampen my rising hysteria.

He huffed out a breath and ran a hand through his hair. "There are some people who want something from me...something I can't give them. They want to use you as leverage." He paused for a moment and squeezed his eyes shut before snapping them open to pin me with an impassioned stare. "They've made an overt threat."

I stumbled back from him, my mind spinning as it tried to take in everything he was saying. "What people?"

"I don't want you knowing more than—"

"What people?" I bit out, more in control of my voice now. "If someone is a danger to me, I deserve to know who."

Marco stood with his fists clenched, his jaw working as he seemed to decide how much he should say. Finally, he acquiesced. "Vito Manzella and his crew."

I plopped down on the couch behind me, my stomach churning like there was a tropical storm gaining momentum inside. "Vito," I whispered.

Marco kneeled down in front of me and took my hands in his. "I don't think he means to follow through on this threat. He's posturing, trying to get what he wants."

"What does he want?" I looked up from where his large hands held mine and into his eyes.

There was a small amount of desperation and fear there; it didn't help me to feel any better. "Something I'm unable to give him at the moment."

"That's bullshit. Tell me what he wants," I demanded. My voice was less controlled than before as panic began to set in.

Marco shook his head. "I can't."

"Why?" I pressed.

"The reasons don't matter."

"Because you're not the one in danger! I realize you just came to town and you might not understand what type of man Vito is, but—"

"I know exactly the kind of man he is." Marco gripped both of my shoulders and leaned in. "And rest assured, I am very much in danger."

"Why is he doing this?"

"He is a serpent. Cold and heartless. Which is why I will not take a chance with your life."

My life. *Oh, God.* What about... "My son," I whispered.

Marco's fingers dug into my shoulders for a brief moment before he removed his hands from me altogether. "What son?" he said flatly.

If the situation wasn't so serious, I'd never be divulging this information to Marco. But he needed to know. "I have a son. He's only nine and he needs me." Tears burned behind my eyes. I wrapped my arms around myself and began rocking back and forth on the couch. "He's sick and needs a lot of care. I'm all he has. What if they hurt my son?!" I shrieked.

Marco stood from kneeling and sat beside me, enveloping me in his arms, whispering for me to calm down. The arms that had made me feel so safe and secure before no longer held the same warmth and feeling of protection.

"It is because of me that you are in danger," he said in a voice laced with guilt. "I will ensure you are *both* safe. I want you with me until I am sure the danger has passed."

"I don't understand, though. Why do they want me? I'm an escort. You're paying for my time. Why would they think that threatening me would sway you to do *anything*?"

Marco released me from his hold and stroked the curve of my jaw with his thumb. "They've been watching us. They can see how much you've come to mean to me."

I held his gaze. How had I allowed myself to get into this situation? I knew exactly how. By letting myself fall for Marco. And by doing so, I'd unknowingly walked into the snake pit.

"Mi dispiace, dolcezza. I'm sorry. Words cannot express how much it pains me that I've put you in this position."

I pushed him away from me and stood from the couch. "I need to think." I started to walk away, but Marco caught my arm and spun me around to face him.

"There is nothing to think about. This is happening. For your own good. And your son's."

Daniel. Shit! "What am I going to tell him? He doesn't know what I do for a living! And I've never even introduced him to a boyfriend before. Now I have to move him in with...with a....client?"

Marco pressed his lips into a thin line. "I am more than that and you know it. You're lying to yourself if you think this thing between us is just business. Why do you insist on denying it?"

What did I say to that? He was right, of course. Even if I had been doing everything in my power to deny the truth. I wrung my hands into my hair. "None of that matters right now! God, I can't even think straight."

"This is what is going to happen," he said in a tone that brooked no argument. "You are going to go home and pack some things for the two of you. You will tell your son whatever you need to, and then you will return here. Anything else you might need, I will have Sal retrieve for you."

I chewed on my bottom lip, a nervous habit I'd had since I was a child. My mother always tried to cure me of it. She'd cringe if she could see me now.

"What about you?" I asked.

His forehead creased. "What about me?"

"How are you going to feel having a kid around all the time? Especially one that requires so much care."

Marco's arms wrapped around my waist. I tried to push him away, but he wasn't having it. "First, you being here all the time will be no hardship. Selfishly, I look forward to it, though I wish it were under different circumstances. Second, just because I do not have a child does not mean I don't like children. I look forward to seeing a different side to you."

"He has lots of appointments. We can't stay in this suite *all* the time."

"Sal will accompany you whenever you must leave here."

"What about all of his medical equipment? And he has a night nurse."

"We will have it all brought here. This nurse...I assume she goes to your house when you're...working?" His voice dropped on the last word like he didn't like thinking of it.

I nodded. "She stays with him while I'm gone in the evenings. Daniel...he thinks I'm a bartender."

Marco gave a curt nod. "Then that's what he will continue to think. You can leave as you normally do and we will spend our evenings out. I'll hire security to watch the suite while we are gone."

This was all way too Double-O-Seven for me. No, my life wasn't typical compared to most people, but I also wasn't used to being on high alert because of a potential attack.

"I don't know, Marco." I chewed on the inside of my lip again.

"Mia cara, I need to know you're safe." He placed a chaste kiss on my lips. "Think of your son. I don't believe him to be in danger, but he needs his mother."

"Isn't there some way to keep us safe in our own home?"

He shook his head. "My suite is much more secure. There's only one point of entry, and the hallways, stairwells and elevators to get up here are all under surveillance by casino security. It's double the protection."

He had a point. "And Leroy?"

Marco tipped his head and looked at me from under drawn eyebrows. "Do you really still feel that he's needed to accompany us out in the evenings?"

"No, but I'd feel better if he was the one to stay and watch the suite while we're out at night. Daniel knows him.

They've met before."

"And you trust this man completely?"

Marco pinned me with a stare that had me questioning Leroy, which was silly. I'd known Leroy a long time, and he'd proven himself trustworthy in the past. More than once he'd put himself in the path of danger to keep me safe.

I nodded. "I'd trust him with my life."

Marco still looked unsure but gave me a slight nod. "I hope you never have to." He pulled me in close and kissed my forehead.

I exhaled and closed my eyes. *So did I.*

CHAPTER EIGHTTEEN

I barely slept after I made it home. Instead, I chose to lie in Daniel's bed with my arms wrapped around him, savoring our last night together in our own home for however long was necessary.

I was nervous as hell about how he'd react when I told him we were moving temporarily. Nothing I was able to come up with in my head sounded like a plausible excuse for why we would suddenly be moving into a hotel suite with a man he'd never met.

Gazing around the room in the early morning light, I took in the artwork Daniel had created over the years that I'd had framed and hung on his wall. It wasn't anything amazing, but it was a sign of what he was capable of when he put his mind to it. Photographs of the two of us were proudly displayed on his dresser, and I remembered every one of those moments with complete clarity. My eyes stung with unshed tears when I realized we'd have to put off redecorating his room. He'd been so excited about it.

Daniel was going to be ripped away from everything he knew and thrown into a strange, new environment. The thought caused anger to well up inside. This was all my fault. My fault for being an escort in the first place. My fault for getting close to Marco.

Yes, I could be angry at Marco, but the reality was that he wasn't the reason I was in danger. In fact, he was doing everything in his power to keep me safe. Marco had refused to reveal to me why he couldn't just give Vito what he wanted, but he swore to me that he had his reasons. I chose to believe him. He'd been sincere, and it'd been obvious that my being in danger was tearing him up. And in my heart, I knew the real reason this was happening was because of Vito.

Daniel stirred in my arms and his eyes fluttered open. "Hey," he said, his voice rough from sleep. He blinked a few times before his gaze settled on my face.

"Morning," I said in a shaky voice. "Did you sleep well?"

"Yeah." He yawned, causing his eyes to water.

Before mine could do the same, I said, "I hate to spring something on you as soon as you open your eyes, but we need to talk."

"Is everything okay?" I detected the concern in his voice, and the only thing I wanted to do was set him at ease.

I adopted the most nonchalant demeanor I could and continued. "Everything's fine, buddy." I mussed his hair to solidify that point. "I got a call from the landlord though, and they've discovered that this house was built with asbestos. It's some very unhealthy stuff if you happen to breathe it in. The landlord wants to remove it all from the house, and it's a big process so we're going to have to move out for a while."

"How long do we have to go?"

"I can't say. Sometimes when they start construction projects like this, they realize there're other problems they have to fix. It could be a while."

He seemed to think about that for a minute…an excruciatingly long minute in which I was unable to read his reaction. "Where are we going to go?"

Deep breath. This was the tricky part. "Good news!" I said with false enthusiasm. "I have a friend that has offered to let us stay with him."

Daniel's eyes narrowed a bit. "What's your friend's name?"

"Marco," I managed to say evenly, though I have no idea how.

"Where does he live?"

I brushed my hand through his hair, needing the contact. "Right now he's staying in a really nice suite at the Bellagio. You and I will share a room, and the hotel can make anything we want to eat and bring it up to us."

"Will Martina still be with me at night until you get home from work?"

"She sure will, buddy." I forced a smile on my face. I'd filled Martina in on the basics when I'd arrived home, letting her know that there were 'some things going on' but skirting the details of *why* we had to relocate temporarily. She'd been more than willing to come to the hotel to care for Daniel, as I knew she would be. She loved my son almost as much as I did.

"Okay. Sounds like fun."

I stared at him, unblinking for a moment, dumbfounded at his reaction. "Do…do you have any more questions?"

His gaze wandered the room for a minute before he responded. "Is Marco your boyfriend?"

I should've seen it coming. It was the obvious question for him to ask, but I'd been so focused on his reaction to us having to leave the only home he'd ever known that the question of who Marco was to me hadn't even registered in my mind.

I weighed my options. I could say he was strictly a friend, but I had no idea what to expect from Marco in front of Daniel. Would he keep a physical distance between us, or would he continue to wrap his arm around me and embrace me? I opted for the middle ground.

"We've been seeing each other, yes."

"Like dating?"

Was that excitement I detected in his voice?

"Like dating," I confirmed.

"That's so awesome, Mom." The smile that lit up his face could have knocked me over. Literally. If I'd been standing, I'm sure I would've stumbled.

"Why are you so excited about that, Daniel?"

He gave me the look that only your child could give—the one that says you are the most dense person in the world. "Mom, you need to get a life. You've never even had a boyfriend."

I brought my hand to my mouth and stifled a laugh. "What are you talking about?"

"You never do anything fun. You're always working or taking care of me. When I see Craig, he's always telling me how his mom has different boyfriends around. I've never seen you with a boyfriend, Mom."

Craig was another child with muscular dystrophy who

we sometimes ran into at the children's hospital. After a while, you got to know the small community of families in the area who were all dealing with the same challenges as you.

"I've been perfectly happy having you as the only man in my life, buddy. Don't ever think differently." I delivered a kiss to his cheek, and for the first time in a long time, he didn't moan and groan about it.

"I know that. But I want you to be happy. Besides, it'll be nice to have a guy around."

Maybe having a male influence—for however long it might be—would turn out to be a good thing for Daniel. I wasn't able to push aside the guilt tugging at my heart over the fact that he'd never had a man in his life.

"Sure it will. Now we have to have a quick breakfast and get on over there so the landlord can get started on what he needs to do here."

"Awesome. Let's get going, Mom. I want to get over to the Bellagio to check this place out."

I ruffled his hair again and got out of bed to begin our usual morning routine. Things were changing, but I was determined to keep to our regular schedule as much as I could in the coming weeks.

Even still, somehow I knew in my gut that once we left this place, nothing would ever be the same.

CHAPTER NINETEEN

Daniel and I arrived at the Bellagio a little before lunch. He seemed to be nothing but excited about the changes that awaited us. The nauseous feeling in my stomach hadn't faded since I'd told Daniel what was going on, and I was so anxious and jittery that I spent the elevator ride up to the suite pacing the small enclosure.

"You're going to make yourself dizzy, Mom," Daniel said, watching me trace the same invisible path around the small square.

"Sorry, buddy." I forced myself to stand beside him, though I wasn't able to keep still. Instead, I jiggled my legs back and forth until the door dinged, signaling our arrival.

With a deep breath, I stepped out onto the bright hallway carpet. Daniel followed me to the suite in his electric wheelchair.

Before I knocked on the door, I bent down and cupped his small face in my hands. "Now listen. If you're uncomfortable here and don't like it for any reason, you say the word and we're gone. We can find somewhere else to stay until we can go home, okay?"

"Okay, Mom. But you worry too much. If you like this guy, I'm sure I will, too."

I gave him a small smile and kissed his cheek without responding. That earned me a glare for once again treating him like a 'baby.'

Finally, I knocked on the door and stood waiting with my arm around the back of his wheelchair. The door opened a moment later, and Marco stood with a charming smile on his face as he took us in, his eyes resting on my son.

"You must be Daniel." His genuine smile radiated warmth. I swear I fell a little more for Marco in that moment. And then he looked at me and said, "Brandi, good to see you again."

Shit.

"Who's Brandi?" Daniel asked. *Of course he did.*

Marco's fists clenched at his side, probably angry at the reminder that I still hadn't shared my real name with him. Daniel looked between Marco and me, waiting on one of us to answer.

"It's just a nickname that Marco calls me. Long story."

Daniel shrugged it off and returned his attention to the man filling the doorway in front of us.

"Thanks for letting us stay at your place," Daniel said. "I've never stayed in a hotel before." His face and his voice radiated excitement, and a small part of me—however fucked up it might be—was thankful for the situation because it meant that I'd been forced out of the protective box I'd constructed. For the first time, I was forced to really let

Daniel live.

"You're more than welcome," Marco said. "Want to head in to check it out?"

"Yeah!" Without warning, Daniel propelled his wheelchair forward and Marco jumped out of his way to let him through the door. Daniel was speeding down the hallway into the living area.

"Daniel, you need to be more careful. You could have run Marco over," I called out after him.

Marco's soft chuckle dragged my gaze back over to him. "I'm fine." He leaned in and pressed a chaste kiss to my lips.

"Still, he needs to watch what he's doing. He could hurt someone."

Marco gazed down at me with an amused grin.

"What?" I asked, scrunching my forehead.

"It's possible you look even more lovely like this." He brushed my hair back from my face.

"Like what?"

"Like this." He gestured to the jeans and cotton tank top I wore. "Less make-up. No expensive dress. A mother. Softer." He leaned in and kissed the top of my head. "Sei una ragazza aqua e sapone."

"What does that mean?"

His thumb brushed against my cheek. "I think Americans might refer to it as 'the girl next door.'"

I let out a humorless laugh. I was most definitely *not* the girl next door, and I'd certainly never had anyone refer to me that way before. "I should go check on Daniel. Who knows what he's getting himself into in there."

"As you wish." He pulled his phone from the pocket of his pants. "I will call Sal to grab everything from your car."

"I'd appreciate that. Thank you."

"No thanks necessary." He bent to give me another quick kiss, which for some asinine reason made me blush like an innocent schoolgirl. *Totally ridiculous.*

I pushed past Marco before he could notice.

When I reached the living area, Daniel had his wheelchair practically pressed up to the glass and was looking down over the small lake that was home to the fountains and the Vegas strip. There wasn't much to see in the daylight, but I knew that come darkness, he wouldn't be able to get enough of the view.

"Well, buddy, what do you think?" I moved to stand beside Daniel and placed my hand on his shoulder.

"This is *so* cool, Mom. I can see all of Vegas up here." I laughed at his exaggeration and soaked in his happiness. The look of pure astonishment might have made it all worth it.

"Wait until you see it at night." Marco approached from behind and stood on the other side of Daniel.

"Where are you from?" Daniel looked curiously up at Marco, who towered above him in his wheelchair.

Marco chuckled. "I'm from Italy. Do you know where that is?"

Daniel nodded as best he was able. "My mom taught me where all the countries in the world are on the map. Italy is in Europe. It's the boot." His voice exhibited his pride at being able to recite the information back to Marco, and I realized that my son was trying to impress him.

"That's right. You're a smart young man, Daniel." He smiled down at him, a warm, content smile that made me wish there was some way for this to be real. "How would you like me to teach you some Italian while you're here?"

"Wow! That would be awesome! Next time I see Craig, I can surprise him. Craig is my friend..." My mind drifted as the two of them continued to talk, and sadness filled the crevices of my fractured soul.

My little boy had never known what it was like to have a father. I'd need to have a talk with Daniel about the fact that this wasn't permanent—and soon. I didn't want him getting ideas in his head that Marco and I would be riding off into the sunset together.

Sal entered the suite, interrupting Marco and Daniel's bonding. Marco turned to face his right-hand man and Daniel spun his wheelchair around.

"Good morning." Sal tilted his head at me and I returned the gesture.

"Sal, this is Daniel." Marco gestured between the two. "Daniel, this is my friend Sal. He works for me."

"Good to meet you, Daniel."

"Hi, Sal." He cocked his head to the side a bit before adding, "That's a funny name, you know. I've never heard it before."

"Daniel!" I admonished.

Sal waved me off with a rare smile. "It's short for Salvatore, but that's such a mouthful that most people just call me Sal."

"Are you from Italy, too?" The extent of Daniel's curiosity both surprised and amused me.

"I am."

"Cool."

Sal gave Daniel a small smile then stared intently at Marco for a moment. The atmosphere in the room changed, the mercury dropping along with my stomach.

"Buddy, why don't you go check out our room? We

even have our own bathroom." I pointed in the direction he should go.

"Awesome!" He moved the joystick for his chair and began wheeling in that direction.

"I'll be there in a few minutes," I called out after him.

Once he was out of earshot, I looked between Marco and Sal. "What's going on?"

Marco spoke up first. "Sal wanted to go over a few things with you. Security precautions."

My palms grew clammy at the reminder of why we were *really* here. "Oh, okay."

"It's important that we're on the same page," Sal said. "When you leave here, it cannot be alone. You need to make sure that you're either with Leroy or myself. You are *not* to be left unattended."

"Got it." I nodded, already knowing this part of it from what Marco had said before.

"I'm going to need to bring Leroy up to speed on everything going on," Sal continued.

Shit. I hadn't thought of that. This entire situation has been such a whirlwind that I hadn't had a chance to consider all the repercussions.

"Okay, I guess. He can fill Sylvia in, too." There was no point in arguing. It was pretty clear that Marco and Sal were running the show and I was just along for the ride.

"I'm also going to need the names of all the people you come into contact with on a regular basis. I understand that Daniel has quite a number of therapists and a night nurse. I'll have background checks done on all of them."

"Isn't that a little invasive? These people have worked with Daniel for years. They'd never do anything to hurt us."

I turned my gaze toward Marco to see him staring at

me intently. "Never underestimate the will of a person to survive. Everyone has a weakness to exploit. Vito won't hesitate to turn those people you trust against you."

I blanched. Marco's statement had me so fixated on whether or not I could trust those people already in our lives that I didn't bother to question whether I could trust the two men in the room with me.

ELISABETH GRACE

CHAPTER TWENTY

The rest of my morning was spent getting us set up in our new room. I made sure all of Daniel's medications had arrived, put both of our clothes in the drawers, and set up his equipment in the bathroom so either Martina or I could help him bathe.

Afterward, I helped Daniel with his lessons at the dining room table while Marco worked on his laptop. He'd gone out of his way to make us feel at home, to the point that he told Daniel he could decide what we were eating for dinner—something I was sure he must be regretting right about now.

I giggled as I watched Marco stab a chicken nugget with a fork and pick up his knife to start cutting it. "Why do you laugh?" he asked, his gaze darting from one side of the table to the other when Daniel began laughing, too.

"You don't use a knife and fork to eat nuggets," Daniel said, his eyes wide and unbelieving.

I reached down and grabbed a nugget off my plate,

ELISABETH GRACE

brought it to my mouth, and took a bite. Daniel and Marco both started laughing at the same time. When I'd swallowed, I asked Marco, "Have you never had a chicken nugget in your life?"

He set his fork and knife down beside the plate and tilted his head before responding. "Suffice to say they're not big in Italy," he deadpanned.

"What do you guys eat over there?" Daniel asked with a mouthful of fries.

"Daniel, don't speak with your mouth full, please," I chided.

Marco shrugged. "A lot of pasta and seafood. Tomorrow night, why don't I order us in something reminiscent of my country and you can try it?"

Daniel grinned. "Awesome! Just not spaghetti, okay? Mom always makes that at home, so I already know what that's like."

Marco and I both chuckled. "No spaghetti. Got it."

I was still curious about who Marco was in his regular life, so I took the opportunity to dig a little further.

"What's your life like back in Italy?" I asked, reaching for my drink.

"Not that different than here. I work a lot but always get over to my Mom's on Sunday for a big feast with the whole family. Since my dad passed away a few years ago, I have very little time for any extra-curricular activities. I make sure to get my workouts in, but my schedule leaves little time to enjoy what life has to offer."

I frowned. "That's a shame. You should make some time for fun in your life." Though Marco hadn't seemed morose when he was describing his life, I'd detected an undercurrent of yearning in his voice. For what, I couldn't be sure.

"You never do anything fun either, Mom," Daniel not-so-helpfully added.

"Gee thanks, buddy." I gave him a smile.

"Well, you don't. If you're not at work, you're home with me." His hand wobbled as he moved it toward his plate to pick up a nugget. It dawned on me that I'd forgotten to grab his assistive cutlery that made it easier for him to hold his utensils. He'd need it tomorrow so I made a mental note to ask Sal about grabbing them from the house for me.

"Seems we both need to get more of a life." Marco grinned then reached across to grip my hand and squeezed.

I rolled my eyes. "I'll have to work on that."

"Do you have any brothers or sisters?" Daniel asked. Mentally, I thanked my son because I'd wondered the same thing.

Marco shook his head. "I am an only child."

"Mom said you guys are dating. Does that mean you're her boyfriend?"

My cheeks heated. Marco opened his mouth to respond, but I cut him off before he was able to say anything that might—in the end—prove more confusing for Daniel.

"Why don't you let Marco finish his dinner and save the twenty questions for later?"

He sighed. "Okay, Mom."

Marco glanced over at me with a warm smile and winked in a completely charming gesture that sent goose bumps trailing up my arms. I returned his smile and pushed back the urge to let him in.

I knew if I released my heart from its rusty cage, it would begin beating again for the man across the table. I also knew that after this was all over, my heart would stutter to a stop and the pain would be catastrophic.

CHAPTER TWENTY-ONE

That night, I pretended to go to work for Daniel's benefit, when in reality Marco and I went downstairs for some light fare and drinks in one of the Bellagio's many restaurants under the watchful eye of Sal. I was a little nervous about leaving Daniel, but Leroy was standing guard outside the suite and Martina was inside. That, in addition to the fact that I was only an elevator ride away, got me out the door.

After eating, we decided to go next door to Hyde, a bar that overlooked the lake and fountain show. Black and white striped pillows mixed with pure white couches, but the glow from the water outside almost made them appear beige. A backlit bar and gray marble floor finished off the space so that it appeared luxurious but not pretentious.

It was busier than expected so there were no seats to be found. I didn't mind. I was content to sip on my glass of wine and make conversation with Marco.

"I wanted to discuss something with you, cara."

"Okay…" The last time Marco had started a conversation this way the news had not been good.

"Our situation has changed. You're living with me now and I no longer feel comfortable paying you for your…services."

Shit. I hadn't even thought about the financial ramifications of moving in with Marco.

"I realize that Sylvia will still demand her cut, but I wondered if we might come to an agreement whereby I deposit funds directly into your account. More like an…allowance of sorts."

I didn't like the idea of feeling like a kept woman, but I liked the idea of Daniel finding out what I did as a result of envelopes of cash being exchanged even less. I also felt the same as Marco. In some strange way the fact that my son and me were now staying with Marco made the exchange of cash every night for services rendered somehow feel wrong.

It was no longer a plain and simple business deal.

"I think that might be for the best," I admitted.

Marco was pleased and leaned in to give me a swift kiss on the lips. "Excellent. Now let's enjoy the rest of our evening.

We moved on to other more pleasant topics, then halfway through my drink, I heard my name being called from behind me.

"Brandi!" I hesitated turning around, knowing that no good could come from someone who was calling me by my working name. "Brandi!"

This time Marco's gaze darted behind me, and when his eyes narrowed ever so slightly, I knew I'd been right to try and avoid whoever it was.

I looked over my shoulder to find Julian approaching us, his sandy-colored hair perfectly mussed up and a big smile on his face. He wore a pair of dark jeans and a black button-down shirt.

"You know this man?" Marco asked, his voice strung tighter than a guitar string.

I nodded, then turned back to face Marco. "He's a..." I paused, unsure how to refer to him. I knew without a doubt that Marco would not be pleased to know Julian was a client. "A friend."

My hesitation was enough. Marco was a smart man. His free hand clenched into a fist, and I was sure I heard a growl escape him over the music playing throughout the room.

Shit. I'd have to do damage control with Marco later. I could only deal with one man at a time.

Remembering Sylvia had said Julian was upset that he couldn't book me, I inhaled a deep breath to calm myself. I turned to face Julian, feeling like I was in the path of a head-on collision.

From the corner of my eye, I noticed Sal emerge from the crowd to stand a few feet away from us. He hadn't made his presence obvious all night, but he must have been assessing the threat now as Julian drew closer.

"Brandi. You look as gorgeous as ever," Julian said when he reached me, slipping a hand around my waist and leaning in to kiss my cheek for a fraction of a second longer than he should have. He pulled back and immediately turned his attention to Marco, who'd now come to stand beside me.

Julian was as attractive as he always was, but the thought of being with him now sent a chill up my spine. And not the sexually satisfying one of promised pleasures to come, but the kind that caused the hair on the back of your neck to stand on end.

I smiled at him, but it felt tense and unnatural. "It's good to see you."

"It's been a while. Too long, really." His gaze drifted up and down my body unabashedly, and I tensed when Marco's hand slipped around my waist. It felt like he was claiming me, and when Julian's gaze darted down to Marco's hand on my hip, I knew I wasn't the only one who'd noticed.

"Julian, this is Marco. Marco, Julian." I kept my voice light and motioned between the two of them, but neither man acknowledged the other except for a brief nod.

"I tried to get a hold of you a little while ago, but I heard you were busy," Julian said. Marco's hand flexed on my hip. "I guess I know why now." Instead of looking at me when he said it, Julian was staring hard at Marco. I didn't have a clue what Marco's expression looked like, nor would I since I was too afraid to glance over at him.

"I've been kind of tied up lately," I responded.

"Literally or figuratively?" Julian asked with a sly grin.

My eyes widened and I almost choked on my tongue. *What the hell was I supposed to say to that?* Rather than respond, I laughed awkwardly, but Julian continued to fan the flames.

"I remember we tried that once. You remember that, right, Brandi?"

What. The. Fuck.

"Um..." My tongue felt ten sizes too big for my mouth in that moment, and I was incapable of speech. Julian may as well have pissed on me to mark his territory.

Marco hadn't said a word, and somehow that scared me more than if he'd lashed out and punched Julian in the face. His quiet intensity only made me think he was more dangerous than ever, a bomb on the verge of exploding.

"I'm just kidding with you." Julian laughed insincerely and winked at him, but he'd already lobbed the grenade—the damage was imminent.

I couldn't continue to talk to Julian in front of Marco. On so many levels it felt wrong. I glanced over to Marco. "Would you excuse us for a moment?" His eyes darkened, appearing murderous as he looked down at me. He didn't even acknowledge that I'd spoken, and I figured that was as good as I was going to get to an agreement.

Stepping forward out of Marco's hold, I tugged on Julian's shirt sleeve and pulled him several feet away from Marco until I was pretty sure he wouldn't be able to hear us over the music. Sal repositioned himself closer to us, though he needn't have bothered. If my hunches about what Julian did for a living were correct, he could protect me as well as Sal.

Julian wore a self-satisfied smirk on his face, and though I wanted to lay into him for approaching me while I was with someone else, I reminded myself that this was business. Brushing off Julian would be akin to losing a great deal of profit—profit I would need after Marco left. He wouldn't be around forever and I'd once again be on my own to support my son and try to make the resource center happen.

"I'm sorry you haven't been able to reach me." I put on my best sympathetic face and placed my hand on his upper arm.

"When will we be able to get together?" he asked and brought his hand up to cup my cheek. "I've missed our time together."

I smiled on the outside. Inside, all I could focus on

was how wrong his hand felt on my face. I wanted to remove it more than anything, but I couldn't bring myself to do it knowing that it could potentially cost me his business.

"I have, too. If you speak with Sylvia, she'll be sure to set something up as soon as I'm available." I could practically feel Marco's stare boring into my back as Julian trailed a path down my cheek, resting his hand where my neck met my shoulder. I just wanted this conversation over and done with, but at the same time I was afraid to face Marco. "Well, it was good seeing you. I'd better get back to my...date."

Julian's lips turned down at the corners before he said anything. "You do that. But we'll be seeing each other soon." He glanced over in Marco's direction before looking back at me. "Count on it." Julian leaned in, but instead of kissing me on the cheek again, he went straight for my lips, placing a quick kiss there before taking off.

I might have spent years as a hooker, but it was the first time I could remember truly feeling like a whore. Here I was making plans to sleep with another man while the man I was currently fucking stood only a few feet away. A part of me despised Marco for it. If it weren't for him and the feelings he drew out of me, it'd be business as usual.

I stood with my eyes squeezed shut...waiting. For what, I didn't know. I knew it wouldn't be good though.

Without a word, Marco snatched my upper arm and dragged me behind him out of the bar.

"Marco, slow down." It was difficult to keep up in my stilettos.

He either didn't hear me or was ignoring me completely, because he didn't falter in his stride for a moment as he led us in the direction of the elevators.

Panic set in. Maybe he was so angry with me that he

was going to send me packing.

"Marco, I can explain."

"Be quiet, Brandi." His voice held enough venom to paralyze me—that is, if he hadn't been dragging me along with him.

"I had to talk to—"

"Silenzio!" he shouted. Even over the cacophony of the slot machines, he managed to draw the attention of some of the patrons we were speeding past.

I wisely kept my mouth shut from that point on. I didn't even ask where it was we were headed when we exited the elevator a few floors down from Marco's suite. He didn't release me from his grip until he had to fish a key card out of his back pocket to open the door to the room.

When the lock beeped, he pushed the door open and held it there. "Get in."

Though his anger was barely restrained, I didn't fear for my safety. I trusted that Marco would never hurt me physically.

I did as he asked and walked into the hotel room. It wasn't nearly as extravagant as his suite, but it was still nicer than an average room.

"What are we doing here?" I asked, flinching slightly when the door slammed shut.

"Who was this Julian?" he asked through clenched teeth, completely ignoring my question.

I sighed and looked across the room at him. "I think you know who he was, Marco." My voice was quiet because saying the words out loud caused shame to settle firmly in the center of my sternum.

Marco ate up the distance between us in three strides. "Did you like his hands on you?" I shook my head. "I need to hear you say it out loud. I want to hear the truth of your words."

"I didn't want his hands on me." My breath was shallow as I admitted what I'd been trying so hard to keep hidden.

"Why?" His dark eyes were searching as he looked down upon me.

"Because they weren't yours."

He bent his head and his lips were on mine seconds after the words had left my mouth. I wrapped my arms around his neck and squeezed him closer to me, wanting to surround myself in everything that was Marco. If I could have crawled inside him and built myself a home there, I would have.

His tongue licked along the seam of my mouth and I opened to him. When our tongues touched, a bolt of pure lust shot through me, which was amplified tenfold when Marco groaned like a desperate man. The warm heat of his tongue coupled with the taste of the alcohol he'd been drinking made me moan. His hands roamed over my back and down to my ass, squeezing and pushing me into his hard body. I was practically climbing up him by the time Marco pulled away.

One of his hands pushed into the hair at the side of my head, and he fixed his dark, penetrating gaze on me. "I loathed seeing another man touch you. It was all I could do to not rip his hands from his body."

I placed my hand on his cheek. "I didn't know what to do."

He brought his forehead down to rest on mine. "I don't know that I'll be able to control myself if it happens again," he said, breathing heavily. "You're mine. Do you understand? I don't care what your fucking job is. *You. Are. Mine.*"

Why was it that I didn't feel like a possession when Marco said those three little words? Quite the opposite—I felt euphoric. Most women probably dreamed of being told three very different words, but when Marco told me I was his, it was like a soothing balm to the jagged scars that life had marked me with.

I'd never belonged to anyone. No man had ever cared enough to want to make me his.

"I want to be yours," I whispered. The steel wall I'd erected around myself had transformed into one built from straw, and Marco was the storm that swept in and blew it all to hell.

"Good, because I'm taking what's mine."

He reached forward to the front of my dress, took one side in each hand and then ripped the delicate fabric down the middle, sending it sailing to the floor. It was violent and possessive, but it might've been the hottest thing anyone had ever done to me.

Our mouths crashed together and we both worked furiously to remove each other's clothing. While our tongues twisted and turned, I pulled Marco's shirt out of his pants and unbuttoned it, eventually pushing it down his arms to reveal his bare chest.

The man had the body of a god, and I ran my hands over the hard valleys and peaks of his olive skin. His hands slid behind my back and unfastened my bra, which I let drop before quickly undoing his belt. Marco's tongue trailed along my jaw line and down my neck, causing shivers to break out over my entire body.

I finally had Marco's pants undone, and I pushed

them down his hips until they fell to the floor on their own. I loved the fact that he never wore underwear. It made things so much easier.

His mouth slammed down on mine, demanding and insistent, and he slipped his tongue back inside. When I wrapped myself around him, his rock-hard erection pressed into my stomach and I grew desperate for the feel of him inside of me.

"Marco," I moaned into his mouth.

His hands slid down either side of me and came to rest on my hips. Without warning, he ripped my lace underwear and left it to fall away. I was really starting to like this brute, caveman shit, but I might have to invest in a cheap, disposable wardrobe.

Marco lifted me like I weighed nothing. I wrapped my legs around his waist, and he wasted no time impaling me onto his hard cock. I cried out with the satisfaction of finally getting what I had so desperately been craving.

With a few short steps, he walked over to the wall and pressed my back against it. His large hands gripped under my thighs and he began jackhammering in and out of me. The delicious friction was almost more than I could bear, and I swear I almost came right then.

He drove into me with the fierce determination of a man possessed, his head buried in the crook of my neck. My nipples rubbed against his chest every time he dipped in and out of me, and it caused a tingling sensation to radiate down from my breasts to my core.

"Your pussy was made for me." His lips moved against my neck as he spoke. "How could it not be when it...feels...this...good." His last few words were accented with vicious thrusts inside of me. "I lose control when I'm with you. No woman has ever had the effect on me that you do, tesoro."

"I've never felt this way," I admitted in what was either a moment of weakness or a moment of strength. I couldn't be sure which.

"E non lo sentirai mai piu."

Before I was able to ask for a translation, he pulled me from the wall while still seated deep inside me. In a few short steps, he was standing at the edge of the bed. He let me fall back slowly, bending and following me down so that he didn't fall out of me.

Thank God, otherwise I might have wept. Nothing felt so right or more real as when he was buried deep within me.

We stayed like that for a moment, him hovering over me like a dark raincloud, gazing down at me with thunder in his eyes, a storm ready to unleash its power. "You must never allow another man to touch you again. Capisci?"

I nodded weakly and jerked my hips, eager to get us back on track.

"Promise me. No man should touch what's mine." He ground out the last word with such passion that I felt branded.

"I promise." I looked directly into his eyes when I said the words—and in that moment, I meant them. Though I had no idea how I could ever keep that promise, I knew that if I had the ability to make it happen, I would.

A satisfied grin pulled up one corner of his mouth. "Brava. Now I prove who you belong to." He began moving slowly, grinding his hips into me, around and around, pulling out just enough to give me a taste of what he was capable of.

A coating of sweat covered him and I had the intense

urge to lean forward and lick every last drop off his skin, just to know what he tasted like and to hold a part of him inside of me.

With Marco standing at the end of the bed, he had use of both of his hands…and he used them well. He brought one hand to my clit and rolled his thumb over it in a lazy motion, while his other hand palmed my breast and twisted my nipple.

I cried out from both the pain and pleasure his hands delivered simultaneously.

"You like that, mia cara?"

"Yes," I said, panting.

Eventually, I could take no more. He'd strung me tighter than a bow, knowing exactly how far to push me without tipping me over the edge.

"Marco, fuck me. Please," I begged.

"Is that not what I am doing?" He swiveled his hips in the same rhythm his thumb teased my clit.

"Please…" I moaned.

"I cannot stand to see you beg. You will get your wish. Let's take care of something first."

He clamped down harder on my nipple and increased the pressure on my clit while still swiveling his hips. Within seconds, my orgasm consumed me.

I screamed his name, but instead of letting me come down from my orgasm, he speared into me full force, hammering in and out while my pussy clenched around his hard length.

We fucked in a frenzy of clinging limbs, audible moans, and dirty words. Marco's hand was around my throat, pushing me down into the bed. I could still breathe, and his physical domination of me unfurled something deep inside that I didn't even know I possessed until that moment—the desire to be *owned* by someone.

For more than a decade, *I* had called all the shots. I had been the sole provider for my son. I had been the one who had to live and die by my decisions. Now I realized that I wished I had someone to take care of *me*.

Italian phrases poured from Marco's lips. I had no idea what he said, but he was so damn sexy when his native language rained down from his tongue.

I squeezed my eyes shut as I basked in Marco's assault—the foreign words falling from his lips, his hand clenched around my throat, the feel of his hard cock igniting every nerve ending as it dragged in and out of me.

He shifted his position so the head of his cock now hit my G-spot with every thrust. I arched below him, the feeling too intense, but he held me in place with the hand still wrapped around my neck.

I exploded like a supernova, shattering any semblance of knowing who or where I was. White light shot across my closed eyelids, and as the orgasm dragged on, I became aware of only one thing—*pleasure*. I had never experienced anything like it.

I wasn't sure how long it took me to come back to myself, but when I did, I realized that Marco's thrusts had become erratic and he himself was close to finishing. He pulled out of me and jerked himself to completion all over the outside of my pussy. There was something oddly satisfying about watching the evidence of our need for each other coat my body.

"Like I said…*mine*." Marco leaned down and kissed me. Then, with one hand between our bodies, he spread his semen between my legs in what felt like a primal act. I wasn't sure if I should be disgusted with myself or not, but it made me completely hot for him again and I wanted to start all over.

"Come. We will shower together and then order room service." Marco extended his other hand to help me up. "I've worked up an appetite."

I took his proffered hand and he raised me up off the bed to stand in front of him. "I can't imagine how you did that," I said with a laugh.

He gazed down at me with an expression I'd never seen before—worship. And I knew that it was more than just physical worship because I felt the connection between us, too. It was soul deep and fathomless and scary as hell.

Without responding, he brought one hand to the back of my head and gently pulled it forward. He placed a chaste kiss on my forehead and held it there for a moment.

"I can't imagine how I was lucky enough to find an angel in a city full of sin." He took my hand and led me to the bathroom, not giving me a chance to respond.

It's a good thing too, or I might have cried. I was no angel, that was the truth, but Marco recognized that deep down I *was* a good person who lived by my own moral code. And though
I'd been with a lot of men he was the first one to ever see into my soul.

It was exactly what made him so dangerous.

CHAPTER TWENTY-TWO

An hour and another orgasm later, we both lay satisfied on the bed, wrapped in bathrobes and enjoying a fruit and antipasto platter while watching the nightly news. I'd figured out during our time together that Marco liked to stay on top of not only me but also what was going on in the world. He was a bit of a news junkie.

He finished off the last of the prosciutto and walked over to place the dish back on the room service cart, not returning until he'd arranged everything on the tray to his exact standards. I giggled as I watched.

He rolled his eyes as he returned to the bed. "Mock me if you will."

"I'm not mocking you. I find it quite charming actually."

He crawled across the mattress, causing it to dip as he approached. "You are lucky I am so fond of you." With his hand behind my head, he pulled me forward, bringing his lips to mine. His tongue licked across my mouth, seeking entrance, and I opened to him. As my tongue slid over his, I drew him into my arms, wrapping them around his hard body. We kissed lazily for some time, content to stay in the moment and not needing to take it any further.

When we eventually pulled apart, Marco rested his forehead against mine. "You kissed me." His voice was a potent mixture of relief and awe.

I laughed. "I've done a lot more than that to you."

He shook his head. "No. You *really* kissed me. Just now and earlier. When I was inside you. Not like before."

I hadn't given it any thought. Since we'd arrived in the room, I hadn't felt the need to hold back that part of me. I stilled and grew tense as the realization struck.

"I hope you're not contemplating taking it back." He kissed my forehead. "Now that I've had a taste of you, I want more." He raised his head, and as if making a point, he placed his lips on mine, his tongue pushing into my mouth. I accepted him, knowing in my heart that it marked a turning point for us but not wanting to examine exactly what that meant.

A soft smile formed on my face. "I'm not taking it back."

He pushed a stray hair back behind my ear. "Perfecto." For a moment we sat like that, gazing into one another's eyes—in search of what, I wasn't sure. Ourselves, the other person, what we were together? Contentment wrapped itself around my soul and a smidgen of joy seeped in...until Marco spoke.

"Will you tell me your real name now?" His voice was soft and cajoling, but my entire body stiffened regardless.

"Marco..." Disappointment flashed in his eyes and my

stomach churned because I was the one who'd put it there. But I still couldn't do it. There was no going back from that. If I told him, I'd be giving him all of me. And I had to wonder if he'd still want me once that happened.

"It is okay." He leaned in and gave me a quick kiss on the lips. "You will tell me when you are ready. When you trust me fully."

"Thank you," I said in a soft voice, grateful that he wasn't going to push the issue.

He rose and positioned himself so that he was sitting against the headboard, legs splayed in front of him. When he patted the space between his legs, I was happy to comply, wanting nothing more than to push away the awkwardness of the moment before.

I sat between his legs, my back to his front, and he wrapped his arms around me. I'd never felt so safe and cared for. My feelings for Marco made me realize that something had been missing in my life. So many years of being on my own had almost made me forget how good it felt when someone cared about you and wanted to take care of you. I had the love of my son, but this was something altogether different.

I relaxed back into Marco, completely content, and we watched TV for a while. I had just about drifted off when the sound of Marco's voice woke me.

"Can I ask you something?" The rumbling from his chest while he spoke radiated into my own.

"Of course," I said on a yawn.

"Why did you first decide to become a prostituta?"

I wanted to laugh a little, wondering if he'd said it in Italian because he thought it'd be less offensive. While his question surprised me, it was a topic I was comfortable talking to him about.

"Growing up, it was just my mom and me. My dad passed away when I was so young that I barely remember him. She didn't really date or anything until I was a teenager. Two things happened when I was sixteen. My mom started dating a guy named Josiah, and I fell in love with Damian."

Marco's arms around me stiffened a fraction, and for some reason a small part of me took pleasure in the fact that my statement had bothered him.

"Josiah and my mom started getting serious, and that's when I began noticing some changes in her. We'd never been religious, but religion was important to Josiah so my mom began attending church every weekend with him. She became really involved in the church and began changing the way she dressed, the way she spoke...basically, Josiah and the church became her priority. She was always pressuring me to attend services with them, but I was a teenager and I wasn't interested." I picked away at the fuzz on my robe as I spoke. I hadn't spoken or thought of this time in my life in forever, and it was more difficult than I'd anticipated.

"About the same time, I met Damian. We became inseparable, and when he told me he loved me, I believed him. Suffice it to say, I was young and had no idea what love really was." I didn't add that, to this day, I still didn't really know. "He convinced me that sleeping together was what people who loved each other do, and so we did—once. Don't get me wrong, I wanted to, but I had no idea at the time how much it would change everything."

I paused, remembering exactly how I'd felt when I first found out I was pregnant—terrified, alone, anxious, ashamed. Marco tightened his arms around me and kissed the top of my head. It was all the encouragement I needed to go on.

"After we slept together, Damian began paying less and less attention to me. When I found out I was pregnant, he refused to take responsibility. He said that we'd only been together the one time, so how could it possibly be his? I was crushed. I'd thought he loved me. I realize now that when you're sixteen and a guy tells you he loves you, you're quick to believe it. Especially if you've never really had a father figure in your life."

"He sounds like a bastard, this Damian," Marco said.

I shrugged. "Maybe. Sometimes I wonder if he really was or whether he was just like me—young and scared."

"Being scared is not an excuse for not taking responsibility for what you did."

"I guess. God knows I didn't have that option."

"What did your mother say when she found out?"

Unshed tears burned behind my eyes. Her reaction had always felt like a bigger betrayal than Damian's.

"She kicked me out under the advisement of Josiah. They called me a sinner, my unborn child a bastard...they told me I wasn't welcome in their home since I couldn't follow the path of the Lord." Though I didn't know it at the time, her actions had cemented my resolve that I would *never* choose a man over my child. *Ever.*

"I can't imagine how scared you must have been." Marco's voice held the sympathy I'd always hoped for from my mother.

"I was sixteen, pregnant, and alone. I had a small amount of money I'd saved from a part-time job, and I stole a stash of cash I knew my mom kept in the house and headed to Vegas." I turned my head to look into his eyes. "I was desperate and needed the money. I naïvely figured there were lots of jobs to be had here, and it wasn't really far from where I lived in Utah. When I first got here, I waited tables and barely made enough to live...if you call living in a tiny, fleabag apartment with no furniture living. I knew that once the baby was born, I was going to have to figure something else out."

"You are a survivor." There was no judgment in his voice; in fact, his tone held a hint of pride.

"There was no choice but to survive. I couldn't think of just myself anymore."

His arms tightened around me. "When did you find out about...Daniel?" The compassion in his voice was almost my undoing.

I sighed. "He was still a baby. Daniel has congenital muscular dystrophy, so the signs of the disease came early in his life. That was when I knew that waiting tables wasn't going to cut it."

"If you have more children, will they...?" he asked cautiously.

I shook my head. "Not likely. After I found out about Daniel's diagnosis, I was tested. I'm not a carrier of the gene that causes MD. They determined that in Daniel's case, his disorder was caused by a spontaneous mutation in his genes." I was quiet for a moment while I pondered admitting to Marco my greatest source of shame. I'd already come this far; I saw no point in holding back. "I wondered for a long time if it was my fault he was sick. If it was because I'd been pregnant so young and my body couldn't handle it, or if it was like my mom had said...I was a sinner and God was punishing me."

"Che schemenza. Nonsense. Sometimes there is no answer to the question 'why.' Sometimes life just fucks you over for no other reason than it can."

I turned my head and nuzzled into the crook of his neck, inhaling the scent of clean soap and pure Marco. He ran his hand through my hair and let me take my time before I got back to my story.

"Daniel's medical expenses started piling up. I knew he was going to need expensive therapies, so I ended up bartending at a strip club. I tried stripping to make more money, but I have two left feet and no ear for rhythm. One night Sylvia came in. I learned afterward that she used to frequent the clubs looking for girls who wanted to make more money. I served her drinks and we connected right away, so I told her about Daniel. She said I had the kind of look men loved, then she offered to teach me what I needed to know to make a lot of money in the business. After thinking about it for a few days, I knew it was my best option." I shrugged. "I've been doing it ever since."

Marco was quiet for a minute before he spoke. I found myself on edge waiting to hear what he had to say. "Do you regret it?"

"No." I didn't need to give it any thought. Sure, I had other dreams for myself, but my job had given me the opportunity to take care of my son and offer him the best medical care possible. Most importantly, I was able to spend my days with Daniel. Like any parent with a sick child, I knew that time was my most valuable commodity. Hooking gave me the gift of being able to spend all the time I wanted with my son, since I had to work very little to make a lot.

Marco was quiet, but I felt his acceptance in the way he cradled me in his arms and kissed the top of my head. After a while, he broke the silence. "Let us not speak of such heavy things."

I pushed away from him and spun around so I sat

facing him with my legs crossed. "Oh no, you're not getting off that easy. I have some questions of my own."

He chuckled. "Now, now, bella. I asked but one question." He held his hand in front of him with his index finger pointed up.

"Actually, you asked one at the beginning of my story and one at the end."

"Semantics."

"Fact."

Marco rolled his eyes, though he seemed amused with me. "Fine. You get two questions."

I broke out in a grin, happy to have the freedom to ask him whatever I wanted. There was so much I wanted to know about the man in front of me. What did he look like when he woke up in the morning? When he fell in love with someone, was he a fan of public displays of affection or did he avoid them at all costs? After an argument, would he admit he was wrong and apologize or be stubborn about it?

But some things you could only know by discovering them, so I opted instead for a question that I thought might give me the most insight into this powerful, complicated, and tight-lipped man.

"What's your relationship like with your parents? I know your dad is deceased, but before he passed."

Marco's jaw flexed, as did the fingers of his hand that lay on top of his thighs. He didn't like the topic, but I took him for a man of his word so I suspected he'd answer anyway.

"My mother and I are very close. You've heard what they say about Italian men and their mothers?" He raised his eyebrow in question.

"Yes."

"That's true for the most part. There's not much I wouldn't do to avoid hurting my mother. She takes great pride in me and my accomplishments, especially because I'm her only child. We speak often, and though at times I could do with a little less motherly interference, I love her very much." A warm smile crossed his face, and I could tell that he was picturing her in his mind.

"And your dad..." I prodded.

"My relationship with my father was much more complicated. Prior to me starting to work with him, things were fine between us. After that, things got...messy."

"Messy how?" I asked.

"The kind of messy that makes it difficult to maintain a good relationship with one another."

I screwed up my face, not understanding what exactly he was getting at. "I don't understand."

"Since I was born, my father had been grooming me to take over the company. There was never any question that I would. And I used to worship the man. As a boy, I looked up to him like he could do no wrong. I wanted nothing more than to be like him. A few months after I began working with him, I discovered some things by accident, and I realized that everything I thought I knew about the man was a lie."

I wanted to pry further and ask exactly what he'd found out, but I decided it didn't matter. Marco wasn't a man that shared easily, and I figured that if I had any hopes of him ever sharing with me again, I'd better not push it.

"I'm sorry. That must have been difficult." I reached forward and took his hand. He nodded slowly and gazed at me with pain in his eyes. "It must have been upsetting for your mom, to see you two like that."

He sighed. "She never knew."

"What?"

"I didn't want to hurt her. It would pain her if she knew we'd had a falling out, but it would crush her if she knew why. So I faked it in front of her…for her sake."

I thought of all the times my gut had told me there was something going on with my own son, even when he insisted he was fine. A mother's intuition was a powerful thing.

"Surely she must have known something was going on."

He shrugged. "I think she may have had her suspicions. If she did, she never mentioned them. Probably assumed it was something to do with the office. Though she was proud of the success mio padre had made of the company, she didn't insert herself into anything business related."

We were both quiet for a beat—me picturing what Marco might have looked like as a little boy and him looking a little melancholy. If I had to guess, I'd say he was reliving some of the moments he had with his father.

"Thank you for sharing with me." I squeezed his hand.

"Non c'e' di che." He gave me a weak smile. "I've never spoken to anyone about what happened with my father. In some ways, it feels good."

"It does."

I'd felt the same when I spoke of my past earlier. Sometimes just saying the words out loud to someone and acknowledging their truth made a difference. You didn't need that person to fix anything or say anything in particular. The fact that they cared enough to *really* listen was enough.

"Now, what is your second question?"

I knew all along what I really wanted to ask, but I'd figured I'd start with the easy question.

"Why won't you tell me what Vito and his men want from you?" The now familiar chill raced across my skin at the mention of Vito's name.

"Because to do so would endanger you further. I won't do that." It was clear from the firm set of his jaw that he wasn't going to budge, but I couldn't help trying one more time.

"Marco, it's me who is in danger. I deserve to know."

His hand shot out and gripped the back of my head, forcing me to look straight into his eyes. "Do you have any idea how much it pains me that you have been dragged into something that has nothing to do with you? I will not be an even bigger bastard by putting you further at risk. All you need to know is that I will keep you safe until all of this is resolved. No one is going to take il mio amore from me."

I sulked for a moment with my arms crossed over my chest, my emotions at war inside me. I still wanted to know—no, I *deserved* to know—exactly what was going on, but I hadn't missed the words that slipped past his tongue. And I was sure it was just that, so I pushed it to the back of my mind.

"Fine then. New question. How long has Sal worked for you, and what exactly is it that he does?"

One corner of his mouth crooked up. "I believe you already had your two questions."

"True. But you wouldn't answer the second one." I raised a brow and stared him down, determined to get more information from him while I had the chance.

He grinned. "All right. Sal has worked for my family since I was a young boy. Originally, he worked by my father's side, and since my father passed away, he now works by my side." He paused, playing with the sheet between his fingers before continuing. "As for what he does, that is more complicated to answer. Essentially, he does whatever I ask of him. Sometimes he is a driver, a bodyguard, a confidante—you name it."

"So he's kind of like a consigliere then?" I'd watched enough Vegas mob movies to know the word.

Marco's mouth formed a thin line and all his movements stopped as if he'd been frozen in place. "He is *like* a consigliere, but he is *not* one. Not the way you are thinking anyway."

"Okay," I said in a small voice. I hadn't meant to anger him.

He reached his hands out in front of him. "Come here." I went willingly, wrapping my arms around his waist and leaning against his chest. I pressed my cheek to his hard pec so that his heartbeat drummed in my ear. "My apologies if I sounded angry. I am not. In the past, people have assumed that because my company is successful and I am from Italy that I must be involved in the mafia. I am *not* that man."

Marco's robe had opened a bit, so I turned my head and placed a kiss on his chest. "I would never think that you were."

His hand stroked my hair and we lay there soaking each other in until it was time for us to return to the suite. Him to his bed, and me to Daniel's. Though we were separated, I still felt his presence in my heart.

CHAPTER TWENTY-THREE

Daniel was up bright and early the next morning, and it took some extra effort to pry myself from bed to help him get ready for the day.

Why was it that kids always got up at the crack of dawn on the days that you could really use the extra sleep?

To my surprise, Marco was already up and dressed when we entered the living area. He was speaking to someone in Italian on his cell phone, but he smiled at us, his dark eyes sparkling. I couldn't help the heat that gathered between my thighs as I remembered reaching the heights of passion even I hadn't known existed until last night.

Daniel and I ate from a breakfast tray that Marco must have had brought up to the suite. He'd even been thoughtful enough to leave out the oversized utensils that Sal had fetched from my house for Daniel to use. By the time we finished eating, Marco was just wrapping up his call.

"My apologies," he said, pulling out a chair to join us at the table. "I have to check in on my business in Italy during their business hours, and then I had to catch up with my mother."

"No need to apologize," I said. "Don't let us pull you from your regular routine."

He smiled. "When you're around, it doesn't feel like pulling me from anything. I think it could be achieved by pushing me with a feather."

My cheeks heated and my gaze darted over to Daniel. He was staring off into space and appeared to be in his own little world. Not that I would've minded him hearing such a sweet sentiment from Marco, I just wasn't used to a man being affectionate with me in front of my son.

"No need to worry," Marco continued after I didn't respond. "I'll be sure everything gets done."

I directed my attention to Daniel, not wanting to get wrapped up in Marco in front of him. If he kept on with such sweet statements, I was likely to drag him into the bedroom and have my way with him.

"Daniel." He turned his head to listen to what I had to say. "I'm going to go take a shower, but I'd like you to finish the math lesson we were working on yesterday. When I'm dressed, I'll look over your work and we'll start a new one if you're ready."

He screwed up his face. "Do I have to, Mom? I wanted to see if I could check out the hotel first."

I pushed my chair back and stood at the edge of the table. "You're too young to go wandering around a casino. School comes first. You know that."

He didn't respond, though it was obvious from the way he wouldn't look directly at me that he wasn't pleased.

After getting Daniel's school supplies set up for him, I took a long, hot shower that did wonders to ease my sore muscles from the previous night's activities. Then I dried my hair and put a little make-up on.

As I headed back to the living area, I heard the murmur of voices. Pausing at the entry to the room, I took in the scene before me. Marco was seated on the couch, and Daniel was in front of him in his wheelchair. They were both laughing about something and looked so different from their usual selves.

Gone was the heavy burden of Daniel's illness that I sometimes saw on his face, and in its place was an innocent young boy full of life with infinite possibilities.

The tension around Marco's jaw had disappeared along with the burden of responsibility that usually weighed heavy on his shoulders. He threw 'his head back in a hearty, carefree laugh reminiscent of an adolescent.

"Try again," Marco said to Daniel when they'd both collected themselves. "Piacere di conoscerti."

"Piacere di conoscerti," Daniel said, attempting to imitate Marco's words. *Not bad.*

"Good job!" Marco reached forward and ruffled Daniel's hair, something I'd done a million times over. The fatherly gesture had appeared so natural and effortless to Marco, and I thought my ovaries might explode. Daniel's face lit up at the attention Marco was paying him, and it was confirmation that my son had been missing out by not having a male figure in his life.

"Let's try the whole thing again," Marco said.

"Okay," Daniel said. "You start."

"Ciao," Marco began.

"Ciao. Mi chiamo Daniel."

"Il mio nome e' Marco."

"Piacere di conoscerti, Marco. Come stai?"

"Sto bene. E tu come stai?"

"Benissimo."

"Bravo, Daniel!"

"We did it!" My son looked as happy as I'd ever seen him, and in that moment I handed over another piece of my heart to the mysterious, complicated man who'd made it happen.

Daniel glanced up and noticed me. "Hey, Mom."

I stepped into the room. "Hey, buddy. What are you two up to?" I took the seat next to Marco on the couch.

"I promised him I'd teach him some Italian phrases if he finished his math before you were done in the shower."

"You got it all done?" I asked Daniel.

"Yep. Marco was just teaching me how to introduce myself in Italian."

"You have a smart young man here." Marco wrapped a hand around my shoulder and pulled me to his side. I stiffened for a moment, only accustomed to a man showing me physical attention when I was working. Then I relaxed as I reminded myself that this wasn't work, and it definitely wasn't just any man.

"I can't argue with that," I said.

"He picked it up quickly."

Daniel grinned at Marco's praise.

"Are you guys going to start speaking Italian now so I won't know what you're saying?" They both laughed and then Marco continued to teach Daniel some translations of common English words and phrases.

I, apparently, did not have the same knack for picking up a new language as my son. Though I tried my best, I couldn't seem to remember what the first word I learned was the second I learned the next word. In the end, I was content to observe their interaction rather than participate.

"All right, buddy. We still have some more lessons to get through today."

"I'll leave you to it then," Marco said.

I smiled at Marco, appreciating the fact that he was backing me up in front of Daniel. "Before I go, I want to ask you something," he said, looking directly at me. "I'd like to take you out for a special evening on Saturday."

"Oh?"

"Mom usually has to work on Saturday nights," Daniel said.

Normally that was true, and for a moment I thought we'd stumbled. But Marco covered flawlessly while my tongue was still stuck in my mouth.

"She has the night off this weekend, so I was planning something extra special. What do you think, Daniel? Does that sound like a good idea?"

"Yeah! Mom never does anything fun."

I huffed out a sigh. "You need to stop with that, buddy. I have plenty of fun."

Marco laughed. "Well, I'm going to help make sure of that."

"You don't have to do that."

Marco patted my knee then stood from the couch. "I know I don't, but I want to." He leaned down and kissed the top of my head. "Daniel, if your mom tells me you did a good job with your school work today, maybe we can go over some words tonight after dinner?"

"That'd be great."

Marco buttoned up the front of his suit and smoothed the dark fabric down his chest. "I have a meeting to attend, but I'll be back later. Sal will be nearby if you need anything."

"What about you?" I asked, concerned for his safety but not wanting to let on in front of Daniel.

He winked. "I'll be fine."

"See ya, Marco," Daniel called out as Marco left the suite.

I turned my attention to my son. "That was nice of him to teach you some Italian."

"Yeah, he's cool." I didn't have much experience in this area, but I figured that was as good an endorsement as you could get from a nine-year-old.

I clapped my hands together in front of me. "All right. Let's get started on your next lesson. You head over to the table and I'll grab everything we need."

I sat on the couch for a moment reflecting on how sometimes the changes you least expect can become the biggest blessings. Daniel was the greatest example of this in my life. I couldn't help wondering if meeting Marco would be another.

CHAPTER TWENTY-FOUR

While Daniel worked away at the dining room table, I sat on the couch with my laptop and pulled up the MLS listings. The property I was interested in was still available, which was a good sign. With everything going on, it'd gone by the wayside for a bit, but now that things had settled and we were developing a new routine, it was the perfect time to make an appointment to view the property.

I called the realtor's office and left a message for him to call, then opened a new tab in my browser to log in to my college course. I was checking the syllabus to see what the required reading was when my phone rang.

I was surprised to see Sylvia's name, and then I remembered the run-in with Julian. He didn't seem like the kind to cause trouble, but it wouldn't be the first time a man's ego caused him to do something out of character.

Looking over my shoulder at my son, I said, "Buddy, this is work. I'm going to take it in the other room, but just shout if you need me."

Daniel didn't look up from his work, but I saw him nod his head.

I rose from the couch and walked toward our bedroom, hitting the green circle on my phone when I was almost there.

"Hey, Sylvia. How are you?" I closed the bedroom door behind me.

I heard her exhale into the phone. "You tell me."

One hand held the phone to my ear and the other rubbed at my temple. "If this is about Julian—"

"What happened with Julian?" She sounded genuinely surprised. There went that theory.

"I ran into him last night while I was with Mr. Valenti, and he wasn't very pleased that he still wasn't able to book me."

"Would you cut the Mr. Valenti crap?" she snapped.

I paused for a moment, unsure what to say. Sylvia and I had always had a great relationship, and she'd never once sounded angry with me—until now.

"What do you mean?" I asked with a trace of hurt in my voice.

"I know you've moved in with him."

Of course she did. I'd known Leroy had told her and I'd meant to call her myself. I guess I had procrastinated too long.

"It was necessary, and it wasn't my idea."

She sighed. Again. "Do you know what the downfall of every working girl I've ever known has been?" I didn't want to know the answer, so I didn't speak. She kept on anyway. "They fall in love with their client."

"I'm not in love with him. That's not why I'm staying

with him." I sat down on the end of the bed.

"I know you well enough to know that you would never have moved your *son* in there if you weren't falling for him."

The truth in her words made me cringe inside. "It's not what you think."

"I know what it is. Which, by the way, I'll be having words with Mr. Valenti for putting you in that position in the first place."

"Please don't do that. Marco has been very good to both Daniel and me."

"So it's Marco now, is it?"

Sylvia might have been an older lady, but she was still sharper than a butter knife.

"Look, it's only temporary, and it was my best option. I'm sure that by the time the situation has resolved itself, he will be sick of me and I'll be back to seeing my other clients."

The words tasted like arsenic in my mouth. The idea of going back to regular visits with other men was slowly and deftly corroding my insides. I pushed the thought away, not willing to deal with it until I absolutely *had* to.

Sylvia was quiet for a moment. I was glad that this was a phone conversation, since I was sure her facial expression would've been one of concern mixed with disappointment.

"Just be careful," she finally said in a quiet voice. "You know as well as I do that the likelihood of this ending well isn't good."

I gripped the phone tighter in my hand. "I'm doing my best."

I ended the call and let my head hang down, defeat washing over me. Because deep down, I knew that my best wasn't going to be good enough.

CHAPTER TWENTY-FIVE

I had a few options to choose from in my wardrobe, but I ended up settling on an electric blue gown with a plunging V in the front that draped perfectly over my hips. The back had a small train for added flair, and I paired it with a diamond necklace and bracelet—of the fake variety. When I'd curled my hair and pinned the dark locks back in a loose bun, I was ready to go.

"You look so pretty, Mom," Daniel said as I left the ensuite bathroom.

Martina was getting him ready for bed. "I've never seen you look lovelier," she added.

"Aw stop, you guys." Heat rushed to my cheeks. "You're going to make me blush."

"You already are, silly," Daniel said.

"Thanks, buddy, that's helpful." I laughed, trying to hide my nerves.

Tonight felt different. This wasn't a business function

I was attending with Marco, and I wasn't pretending to head to work for Daniel's benefit. Tonight was about Marco and me without any pretenses or excuses for us being together.

"Marco is waiting for you in the living room," Martina said as she grabbed some pajamas out of the drawer for Daniel.

I took a deep breath. "Okay, I'm going to head out then. Daniel, you be good for Martina, and no trouble at bedtime."

"I'm always good, Mom."

I walked toward him. "I know you are, buddy, but it's my job to always remind you." I ruffled his hair and leaned down for a kiss, but he jerked back.

"Your lipstick," he said with distaste.

I smiled and settled for a hug. "I'll see you in the morning."

I left the room and shut the door behind me. Marco's back was to me as he gazed out the large windows. He must've been deep in thought because he wasn't aware of my presence until I'd almost reached him.

He looked over his shoulder and smiled, then turned around to fully face me.

Wow. Marco in a tuxedo was just...*wow.* Heat pooled between my legs as I took in his broad shoulders and the way the pants tapered perfectly down his powerful legs. He looked every bit the wealthy, powerful, beautiful man that he was.

I held my arms out at my side. "Well, what do you think?"

He growled, and the sound lit up every one of my erogenous zones like they were beacons trying to call him home. "I think we should get going before I pin you down on the floor and we don't make it out of this room tonight." His gaze raked over me again, and the glint of humor left his eyes to be replaced with pure rapture. "I've never seen a woman look as stunning as you do right now. Sei bellissima. Il blu e' decisamente il tuo colore."

"In English?" I wasn't conceited, but I wanted to understand every word he was saying because they felt like a gift he was giving just to me.

"I said that you are magnificent and that blue is definitely your color."

"Oh, well...thank you." I looked down as I felt a blush creep into my cheeks. Again.

Marco closed the distance between us and tilted my chin up with his finger. "I'm excited to take you out this evening." He leaned in to kiss me and I pulled my head back.

"Watch my lipstick," I said, smiling at the reminder of Daniel's reprimand.

Marco blinked as if the thought hadn't occurred to him. "Ah, yes. While it looks wonderful, the fact that it prevents me from devouring you almost makes me want to get rid of it." He paused for a moment, his gaze wandering over my face. "What is that English saying...all things to those that wait?"

I chuckled. "Good things come to those who wait."

"Ah, yes. Or in this case, the *best* things will come to those who wait. How fortunate that I am a patient man." He winked then leaned down to whisper in my ear. "I can't wait to see where those lipstick stains end up though."

My nipples perked up under my dress, begging for attention he couldn't deliver. Not right now anyway.

He grinned down at me with a satisfied smile, as if he knew exactly what he was doing to me.

I cleared my throat. "Are you going to tell me where we're going now?"

He shook his head. "I want it to be a surprise."

I fingered the necklace that lay on my chest. "Well, I look forward to see what you have planned. Thank you."

I held his gaze, though the intensity in his fathomless eyes made me want to turn away.

"Non c'e' di che. You're welcome." He extended his arm and asked, "Shall we?"

"Absolutely," I said, looping my arm through his.

We entered the hallway to find Sal and Leroy talking. In typical Leroy fashion, he gave a long, low whistle. "Baby girl, you are looking F-I-N-E this evening."

I laughed. "Thanks."

"Belissima," Sal agreed with a smile, something I rarely saw from the man.

"If you two are finished ogling my woman, we're ready to leave," Marco said. I didn't think he was really upset at either of the men, but there was the slightest edge to his voice that told me he didn't appreciate the extra attention the men were paying me. I, on the other hand, was trying hard not to focus on what it felt like to have Marco refer to me as *his woman*. Surely he didn't mean it the way it sounded.

"I'll keep an eye on things here," Leroy said. Unease swept over me at the reminder that someone wanted to use me to get to Marco. And the only way anyone could really get to me was through my son.

Marco must have been able to sense my apprehension because he squeezed my hand while he and Sal spoke in Italian.

"Thanks, Leroy." I smiled at one of the few people I trusted with all my heart.

"Don't you worry about a thing, baby girl. Nothing's going to go down on my watch."

I knew he'd protect Daniel and Martina at all costs, which was the only reason I was able to leave the building at all. That, and the fact that Daniel had never actually been threatened. I made a mental note to get some more information from Marco this evening. Whenever I'd brought up the threat to me in the past, he'd quickly shoved off my concern and moved on to another topic. I wouldn't allow that to happen tonight.

"Let us go," Marco said. "I do not want to be late."

I smiled at Leroy over my shoulder as Marco and I walked away, hand in hand. "Still not going to tell me where we're headed?" I asked as we followed Sal into the elevator.

Marco brought my hand to his mouth and kissed my knuckles. "So impatient."

I rolled my eyes and shook my head good-naturedly.

"Let's see how you react next time I try to keep something from you."

He squeezed my hand. "Hmm. That's not funny." From the tone of his voice, I knew he wasn't kidding around any longer.

We sat in the back of the blacked-out SUV as Sal drove us to our destination. I was giddy with excitement to see what Marco had planned. It didn't even matter to me what it was. The mere fact that he'd gone out of his way to do something so thoughtful had me swooning like a schoolgirl.

I quietly observed the direction we were headed and attempted to list in my mind all of the places we might be driving to. Figuring now was as good a time as any for a conversation I knew Marco wouldn't be open to, I drew in a deep breath and asked the question I really wanted answered.

"Have you heard anything more from Vito's men?" Marco's jaw tightened and his hands clenched in his lap. "Marco?"

"Must we speak of such unsavory topics on a night when all I want to do is put a smile on your face and my cock in your pussy?" He reached out and took my hand in his.

I ignored my body's reaction to his words. "We must. I'm tired of not getting any answers to my questions."

His jaw twitched again and I waited, knowing that whoever broke the silence first would lose. Finally, he gave in to my demand. "There has been no outward threat made since the original one, nor have his people contacted me with further demands."

A tiny seedling of hope bloomed in my chest. "That's a good thing then, right?"

"That remains to be seen. It doesn't mean we don't have to be careful."

"How will we know when it's safe for me to return home?"

"So eager to leave me, are you?" he asked in a wry tone.

"That's not what I meant."

He turned his gaze from me to the window. "I'll know."

"But how?"

He sighed and swung around on the seat to face me. "I have people with their ear to the ground. When the time comes, I'll know." His tone was firm and final, so I didn't press him any further. I trusted him and the words he was saying, however foolish that seemed. "Now, can we have a nice evening together and forget all this?" He reached for my hand and brought it to his lips.

I gave him a soft smile. "Of course."

A moment later we pulled up in front of a large cream-colored building with a sprawling front lawn lined with palm trees. The entire scene was beautiful with lights along the pathway that cut through the lawn, more lights strung around the palm trees, and sconces situated on the second floor of the building.

"Is this the Smith Center?" I asked. I'd seen pictures of the building on the news a few years back when it first opened, but I'd never seen the real thing.

"It is."

Sal opened the door for Marco, who exited the vehicle without any further explanation. I shimmied over on the seat so I wouldn't have to exit into traffic, and Marco extended his hand to help me out. "And? What are we doing here?" The words left my mouth before my foot even hit the sidewalk.

"When I am in Italy, I enjoy going to the opera. I thought you might as well."

"Really?" A wide grin broke out on my face.

He chuckled. "Really. Have you been before?" I shook my head. "Excellent. I get a first with you all to myself." He turned his attention to Sal, fired off some Italian, and before I knew it, Sal jumped back in the vehicle. "He will park the car and wait for us in the lobby."

Marco took my hand in his and we started walking up the long path to the entrance. I was so content in the moment that I leaned into him as we strolled past a large sculpture. It felt like I was living someone else's life...like this was all a dream.

Even better than a dream really, since I'd never imagined myself going to the opera. Marco listened to a lot of classical music and opera, and I'd become accustomed to hearing it playing in his suite. I couldn't wait to see an actual live performance.

We entered the building to find the lobby full of people dressed in their finest. Men lounged in tuxedos and the women showed off a plethora of gorgeous evening gowns.

"Would you like a drink?" Marco asked me.

"A glass of wine would be nice."

"Merlot, I presume?" He raised a brow. Since I'd moved into the suite, he'd learned that the rich red wine was my drink of choice.

"Please." Marco led us in the direction of the bar and we situated ourselves in line behind a few other people.

"What opera are we seeing tonight?"

I thought I saw something pass over his expression, but it was gone before I could pinpoint what it meant. "*La Traviata*. It was always one of my favorites."

"Is it in Italian?" He nodded with a smirk. "You might have to translate for me."

He leaned in and spoke into my ear. "I think you'll be able to follow along." Between the smell of his cologne and the cadence of his deep voice laced with his foreign accent, a full body shiver raced through me.

Once Marco had purchased our drinks, we went in search of our seats, which were located in one of the private upper tier boxes directly across from the stage. He told me that most people liked the boxes closest to the stage, but that he'd always preferred those directly across from the stage so he had a more balanced view of the performance. I didn't know anything about the opera, so I took his word for it.

I'd only just taken a seat in the plush velvet chair when the lights dimmed a bit and then went back to normal. Then they did it again.

"Why are the lights doing that?" I asked.

"The show is about to start. The same thing will happen in between acts to let the audience know to make their way to their seats." His response was perfect, not at all making me feel like the uncultured commoner that I was.

"Thank you for bringing me here tonight, Marco. It's all..."

He leaned over and kissed me on the lips. I giggled when he pulled away and I saw that some of the red from my lipstick had transferred to him.

"What is so funny?"

I placed my thumb on his bottom lip and wiped away the lipstick. "I left a mark, that's all."

His hand wrapped around my wrist and held me still. "Of that there is no doubt." Slowly, he guided my hand down and placed it on his chest over his heart.

Our gazes were still locked when the theater plunged into darkness.

I'd been mesmerized during the first act by the richness of the costumes, the sound of the voices echoing through the theater, and the symphony of instruments that filled the space.

"Well?" Marco asked when the lights went up at the first break.

"It's magnificent." I continued to stare at the stage, unable to pull my eyes away from it. "Why did she reject him at first?" I was referring to the main character, Violetta, who had refused the advances of her true love, Alfredo.

Marco's finger softly turned my chin to face him. "You know what Violetta is?" he asked, his voice serious. I nodded. She was a prostitute, or a *'kept lady,'* from what I'd been able to decipher. "She thought that the only thing that could make her happy was money, and assumed that because of her lifestyle, he could never truly love her."

A knot tightened in my stomach that I didn't even know was there.

"What do you think about that?" he asked, holding my stare.

"I think she has a good point."

A small smile crossed Marco's face, but there was a trace of disappointment there too. "Those are merely obstacles to jump over, not walls erected to keep from moving forward." He leaned in and brushed his lips softly across mine, careful this time not to transfer my lipstick to him. "Now would you like another glass of wine or do you need to use the restroom?"

"Both, please." He nodded then helped me up out of my chair. "Thank you."

When we stepped out into the hallway, I immediately saw Sal waiting for us. He and Marco spoke in rapid Italian to each other. I'd stopped trying to figure out what they were saying weeks ago. I might have been picking up a few key phrases that Marco used often, but when they spoke like this, I could barely tell where one word ended and the other one began.

"Sal will accompany you to the ladies' room while I go get our drinks. I'll meet you back at our seats."

I wanted to tell Marco that I was a big girl and could make it to the bathroom myself, but I knew he'd only tell me he wasn't taking any risks with me, blah, blah, blah. So instead, I just smiled and agreed.

"How are you enjoying the opera?" Sal asked as we worked our way through the crowd.

"I love it. It's like nothing I've ever seen before."

Sal smiled down at me. "It is one of a kind, yes."

He pushed through the crowd, and before I was able to stop myself, I blurted out the question I often wondered when I was around him.

"Do you like me, Sal?" I was never able to get a good read on him. He was always respectful toward me but never outwardly friendly, and I'd never gotten the impression that he particularly liked me.

Surprise registered on his face before he schooled his features. "Why would you ask such a thing?"

"Come on. It's clear that you care for Marco."

He looked over at me and gave me a firm nod. "I have worked for his family for many years."

"That's exactly my point. You can't be happy about the fact that he's shacked up with an escort and her son who you now have to babysit all the time."

We'd finally reached the ladies' room, and thank God the line wasn't too long. When we stopped, Sal rested his hands on each of my shoulders to make sure I was looking right at him before he spoke.

"I have known Marco since he was a small boy. Though some would say he had it easy growing up because of all the resources at his disposal, he also had a lot of expectations put on his shoulders. The only woman he's ever wanted to make happy is his mother...until you."

Sal paused for a moment seeming to debate something internally and finally continued. "You've been good for him. You've given him something besides work to care about. So, to answer your question, yes, I like you. Marco is like a son to me, and you are the woman with whom he is very much taken. And for good reason."

Then he winked at me. Without thinking, I sprung forward and wrapped my arms around Sal, trapping him in a fierce hug, which he eventually returned. "Thank you," I whispered over the murmur of the crowd around us.

When I pulled back, Sal patted my cheek in what felt like a fatherly gesture. "Go see about your business and I'll wait for you here."

I did as he said and then we made our way back through the dwindling crowd in the hall. "You go on in to your seats, and I'll keep an eye on things out here," he said when we reached the entrance to our private booth.

"Thanks, Sal." I think we both knew that I was thanking him for more than just escorting me back to my seat.

I went inside our booth, but instead of taking my seat right away, I stood at the edge of the balcony to get a view of the entire theater. It wasn't an old building, but it somehow still held a charm about it reminiscent of decades past. The space was a mix of wood and soft beige tones, but my favorite part was the roof in the center of the ceiling, which consisted of tiered arches that reminded me of the dome at the top of the U.S. Capitol Building.

I was content and happy awaiting Marco's return when, without warning, the hair on the back of my neck stood on end, and shortly after, the hair on my arms followed suit. I had the distinct feeling that someone was watching me.

My gaze scanned the crowd below and the private sections on either side of the theater, but there were too many people for me to make out anyone who seemed to be paying me any extra attention.

Still, instead of passing, the feeling seemed to be like a snowball rolling down a hill, gathering speed and size and weight as it went, ready to crush whatever lay in wait at the bottom.

My hand moved to my chest as I drew shaky breaths into my lungs in an attempt to calm my racing heart.

"Here you are."

I yelped and spun to find Marco standing behind me, holding my glass of wine. I pressed my hand harder against my chest. "I'm sorry. You scared me."

Marco's forehead crinkled. "Are you okay? You look a little pale."

"I'm fine, yes. Thank you." I took the glass from Marco and swallowed a healthy sip.

I was being ridiculous. There was no reason to think that someone was watching me. They'd have to be crazy to consider trying anything nefarious while I was in the company of Marco *and* Sal. Besides, Marco said earlier that no further threats had been made.

To ease my mind, I took my seat and quickly fired off a text to Martina to make sure everything was okay back at the suite. She responded immediately that they were fine. Daniel had gone to bed without any problems and she said not to worry.

"You sure you're okay?" Marco asked when he took his seat beside me.

"Absolutely," I said and leaned over to give him a kiss, uncaring if it resulted in him wearing my lipstick again.

He smiled at me when I pulled away, and that was the last thing I saw before the lights went down and the second act began.

The next portion of the opera was as spellbinding as the first, and we opted to stay seated during the break, swiveling both our chairs to face one another.

"What does *La Traviata* mean?" I'd been able to follow along with most of what happened in the performance, but I hadn't thought until now to ask what the title meant.

Marco finished swallowing a mouthful of his drink before responding. "It means, '*the fallen woman.*'"

I pressed my lips together and refrained from making a joke at my own expense, because I knew he wouldn't like it. "Why was Alfredo throwing money at Violetta at the party?"

Marco sighed and rubbed the back of his neck. "When Alfredo's father visited Violetta, he told her of Alfredo's sister, who was supposed to marry. Because of Alfredo's relationship with Violetta, the sister was no longer seen as suitable. Violetta thought she was doing what was best for Alfredo when she left him. When she arrived at the party with the Baron, Alfredo questioned whether she loved the Baron. She lied and told him she did. In his fury, he threw the money at her and said that he had paid for all he owed, implying that their time together was an act of commerce rather than love."

I laughed without humor. "Good thing we started this relationship out with commerce first." The words were out of my mouth before I could stop myself. I'd only meant to think them, not voice them. *Damn wine.*

Marco grabbed my wrist and pinned me with a stare that left me afraid to even blink. "Never do that. I will not allow you to devalue what is between us. *Ever.* Do you understand?"

Tears burned in the corners of my eyes, but I nodded. I didn't know if I was emotional because of the ferociousness of his words, or if it was because it was clear that he meant them.

"I'm sorry." Marco's hand cupped my face and stroked it with his thumb. "I did not mean to scare you. I cannot stand when I hear you speak like that about us."

"Can I ask you something without you getting angry?" His jaw ticked, but he nodded his consent. "What do you think your mother would say if she knew you were here with me right now?" I'm not sure why his mother came to mind in that moment, but I was curious to hear his answer.

His palm fell from my face and he reached for my hands that sat in my lap. "I cannot lie and say that if she knew how you made your living that she'd be pleased. But I don't plan on telling her. I know that when she meets you, she will tell me how beautiful you are, she will see what an intelligent woman you are, and she will see what a fantastic mother you are. She will see that you are kind and caring and compassionate. And because of all those things and many more that I don't have time to list, she will know that you are perfect for me."

This man was too much to be believed. The words he said to me, the things he made me feel…they were more than I'd ever dreamed. Even more unbelievable was that it was all starting to feel real.

Marco threaded his hands in my hair and brought his lips to mine in a passionate kiss. I melted into him and tried to pour everything I had into that kiss. My hands roamed his solid back and played with the hair at the nape of his neck. I was vaguely aware of the sound of instruments and the flashing of lights indicating that Act Three was about to start.

The theater went dark, and Marco's hand trailed a path along the outside of my thigh and over the top of my dress. I couldn't help but arch into him, wanting his hands on me—and even better, *in* me.

The orchestra struck up a song, and moments later the powerful voice of the tenor filled the large room. "Marco," I said as his mouth left mine and he ran his tongue along the column of my neck. I patted him on the back to try and get his attention, but he was having none of it.

I opened my eyes to sneak a peek at the theater. No one was paying us any attention. We were unable to see our neighbors on either side, and unless someone in the audience turned all the way around, looking up and back, they'd stand no chance in catching us. Even then they could only see from my shoulders up with the darkness surrounding us.

Marco's warm hands moved underneath my dress and skirted along the skin of my calves, causing me to start. He moved his mouth up to my ear, and in a loud whisper so only I could hear him, he said, "Relax, cara. I'm going to make sure your first opera is a memorable one."

My nipples peaked under the expensive fabric of my dress, and I bit my bottom lip to keep myself from moaning. His hands moved all the way up to my hips, and then he tugged me forward so my ass was at the edge of the chair. I leaned back into the plush velvet of my seat as one of his hands delved between my thighs, pulling my underwear to the side.

When he dipped his fingers into the wetness between my slick folds, I bit my lower lip and moaned. I felt the vibration in my throat, but the only thing I could hear was the tenor's voice resonating throughout the room.

Marco teased me, skimming his fingers briefly over my clit and then sliding them down to my slit but never penetrating. I silently begged him with my eyes. The bastard knew I was desperate. It was clear in the way one corner of his mouth had twitched up as he watched my every reaction to what he was doing.

Finally, he pushed two fingers into me and used the pad of his thumb to stroke my clit. Sweat broke out at my temple as he dragged his fingers in and out, and the sensation of my impending orgasm bore down on me. I lifted my hips to meet his thrusts, uncaring if someone watching the show turned around and my movements gave away our activities.

Marco curled his fingers inside of me to press on the spot that always caused bliss to spiral throughout my body like a raging windstorm, and I came on his hand just as the final notes of the aria surrounded us.

As promised, my first opera was nothing short of memorable.

CHAPTER TWENTY-SIX

I was on cloud nine for several days after the night of the opera. I couldn't help but feel the change in our relationship, and there were times that I completely forgot how we met or why we were staying in Marco's suite. The three of us had settled into a routine, and both Daniel and Marco seemed to enjoy spending time together.

"Do you think Marco will teach me some more Italian if I finish this worksheet before he gets back from the gym?"

I looked up from my laptop screen and across the table at Daniel. "As long as he doesn't have any work to do, I'm sure he'd be happy to."

Daniel's lessons were coming along nicely. He seemed to have a real knack for picking up a new language, so much so that there were times he and Marco would speak in Italian to each other and I wouldn't know what they were saying. I'm pretty sure it was all basic stuff, but my son impressed me nonetheless.

I glanced down at my phone to check the time. Marco would probably be working out downstairs for at least another hour.

I startled when my phone buzzed in my hand and rang with a number that I didn't recognize. "Hello," I answered.

"Hi there, this is Brian Carlisle with Red Rock Realtors. I think you left me a message last week about wanting to see one of my listings."

I immediately perked up in my seat, drawing Daniel's attention. "Oh, you're the one with the listing on Sunset Street?"

"That's me. Sorry I didn't get back to you sooner. I was out of town, and I didn't find out that the person covering for me wasn't returning messages until I got back to the office."

"No problem. I appreciate you calling me now. Is there a chance I'd be able to walk through the building to see if it meets my needs? On paper, everything looks great, but I'd like to see the layout and condition of the place."

"My schedule is swamped since I'm playing catch up, but I was planning on going by there in a few minutes just to check on the property. It's empty, and I want to make sure everything is as it should be since I was gone for a week. Any chance you can meet me down there shortly?"

I figured I could make it work. "Sure. I can leave here in five or ten minutes. Please don't leave if you get there before me."

"All right. Then I'll see you down there in a bit."

"Thanks so much, Brian. See you soon."

I hung up the phone and sprung up out of my chair,

excitement making my stomach tingle.

"Who was that, Mom?"

"You remember the building we drove by a while ago? That was the realtor that has it listed, and he said he can show it to me right now. Are you going to be okay if I have Leroy come hang with you for an hour or so? That way you can finish your work before Marco gets back."

"Sure." Daniel didn't seem bothered by the fact that I wasn't including him, which was good. I had no idea what shape the building was in or whether all the floors would be handicap accessible for our tour.

I dialed Sal, knowing he normally didn't accompany Marco when he went to the casino's gym. The Bellagio wasn't a fortress exactly, but casinos were known for having eyes on everything at all times. The chance of a threat to any of us was probably at its lowest while we were here, and Marco seemed pretty confident that he could take care of himself between the suite and the gym.

Sal agreed to drive me over, and then I poked my head in the hall and asked Leroy if he'd come in and hang out with Daniel until either Marco or I returned. It wasn't as if they didn't know each other. The only reason Leroy was stationed outside rather than inside the suite was to keep Daniel from asking probing questions.

Five minutes later Sal was driving me to the site that might very well be where my dream comes to fruition someday.

Brian was waiting for me just inside the doors when we arrived. He was a frumpy little man with a potbelly and a receding hairline, but he seemed nice enough.

"This is Sal," I said, gesturing in the direction of the

man who had become my constant shadow.

"Pleasure to meet you." The two men shook hands.

"Why don't we head in? I've been through the place already and turned all the lights on, so we're good to go."

"Sounds great." We stepped further into the building, and even though I'd told myself not to bother getting too excited, it was hard not to. The front room was spacious and already had a desk set-up that could act as a reception area. There were no chairs in the room, the tiles were badly worn, and the walls were pretty dingy, but all I saw was potential— the potential to help deserving families.

Brian showed us around the rest of the main floor, which had a few medium-sized rooms and a small kitchen the previous staff must have used. The appliances were old and less than appealing, but he insisted they worked.

"We can't use the elevator since the current owner hasn't kept up on the safety inspections for it, but I'm told that it was in working order when the old tenants left the building."

"Can we use the stairs?" I asked.

"Yep. There's a set at the front of the building and one here at the back. Follow me." He led us through a heavy metal door, and into a stairwell.

"Should we start on the second floor and work our way up?" I asked.

"Sure thing."

We all headed up the stairs, our footsteps echoing through the stairwell. If I'd been alone, I might have been a little freaked out. The lighting cast shadows all over the place, and a few of the florescent lights buzzed and flickered.

By the time we reached the fourth floor, I'd imagined how to best use all the space in the building if I were able to purchase it.

"This level has the largest rooms of the entire place—
" Brian stopped speaking when the blare of a car alarm
sounded from outside.

Sal stepped over to the window and peered out.
"Figlio di puttana."

"Is everything okay?" I asked.

"I think someone was fucking with the vehicle. The
alarm is going off." He glanced at me then back out the
window, deciding what to do.

I waved him off. "Go. I'll be fine."

"Don't go anywhere. I'll be back in a minute." Sal
pinned me with a stare and his gaze darted briefly in Brian's
direction before he raced out of the room.

"Protective, isn't he?" Brian joked.

I just smiled in return.

"This area isn't known to be a bad one. I'm sure it's
an isolated incident." Brian's statement reeked of someone
looking to score a commission.

"I'm not too concerned about it," I assured him.

We stood waiting for Sal to return when the entire
room went black. I turned toward the door and saw that the
once lit hallway was also dark.

"Damn it. You stay here. I'll head down to check out
the panel. I don't want you falling and hurting yourself."

"Okay." I wasn't about to go exploring an unfamiliar
building with no lights and a man I didn't know.

"The last thing I need is another insurance claim,"
Brian grumbled as he used his cell phone to lead the way
toward the exit.

It wasn't pitch black in the room, but it was a rare
cloudy day in Vegas and the windows weren't huge, so my

eyes still had trouble adjusting to the change.

I walked over to the window and saw Sal just getting to the SUV.

That's when I heard it.

Footsteps.

I held my breath for a second and tilted my head, wondering if I was just imagining things. My heart pounded in my chest like a war drum, making it hard to hear anything else.

But no, there was nothing.

I exhaled a relieved breath then dug into my purse to look for my cell phone. The moment my hand closed around my phone, I heard the sound again.

Those were definitely footsteps and they sounded closer this time.

"Hello?" I called out with a shaky voice.

No answer.

The hair on my arms rose, and my breathing became rapid and shallow. I looked out the window and saw Sal still poking around the car.

"Hello?" I called out again.

Nothing.

Surely Brian would answer if it were him.

Wait. There.

That was definitely a footstep—as if someone were trying to move and keep quiet.

Tears sprung to my eyes and I drew in a deep breath, hoping the oxygen would somehow make me brave.

One. Two. Three.

I bolted from the room at the same time I pressed the button to turn my phone's light on. I veered right when I exited the doorway, not bothering to look the other way to see who was lurking. I just wanted to get the hell out of there.

I pushed through the large metal door and into the stairwell, then raced down the stairs as fast I as I could without tumbling to my death, the light from my phone haphazardly bouncing off the walls. When I'd almost reached the second level, the metal door leading from one of the floors into the stairwell opened, followed by footsteps pounding down the stairs.

I didn't bother calling out to see if it was Sal or Brian. My brain was screaming *'run'*, so I ran.

A small sound of relief escaped me when I reached the landing on the first floor, but it was too soon to celebrate. I fumbled to get the door open as the sound of the footsteps on the stairs seemed to grow louder and louder until it was all I heard.

With one final push on the handle, the door swung open into the hallway and I ran blindly toward the front door with tears streaking down my face. When I shoved through the front doors, I immediately inhaled a lungful of fresh air, but in my panic it didn't feel like enough so I did it again. And again.

Sal's eyes grew wide, and he ran over to where I stood.

"What happened?" Concern was etched in every one of his features, but he didn't appear to be panicked like I was. How was he able to keep it together like that?

When I was able to get a proper breath and my heart no longer felt like it was going to burst out of my chest, I explained what had happened with the lights and what I'd heard after.

"Cazzo." He reached into his suit jacket. I didn't even want to know what for. "You go to the car and don't get out until I return."

"No!" I put a hand on his arm. "Please don't leave me here by myself. Let's just get out of here."

He struggled with what to do, his gaze darting between me and the door to the building several times.

"Oh, here you are." I turned and saw Brian exiting the building. "I thought maybe you'd left."

I wiped my tears off my face quickly before Brian could ask about them. "No, I have somewhere to be so we need to get going."

A small frown formed on Brian's face. "I assure you nothing like that has ever happened with the building before. I can't figure out what the hell the issue is, but I'll let the owner know about it and he'll see to it that everything is in working order."

I nodded. "Sure. Don't worry about it." Sal's hand clamped down on my upper arm and he led me toward the SUV. "I'll be in touch about the building," I called out over my shoulder.

Sal deposited me in the backseat then hurried around to the driver's side. He got in, started the vehicle, and pulled away in what seemed like one fluid motion.

My knee bounced incessantly as we drove across town. "Maybe I didn't really hear anything. I could've just been freaking myself out."

"Never ignore your instincts. God gave them to you for a reason."

I nodded, knowing he was right. My instincts had served me well so far. There were lots of times I'd had to rely on them to get me out of sticky situations with clients.

"I should not have left you alone in that building." He sounded angry, and it didn't dawn on me until then that he might catch flak from Marco for what had happened.

"I don't suppose there's any way I can convince you not to tell Marco about this?"

His gaze darted to mine in the rearview mirror, and he held my stare for a beat before his eyes shifted to the road ahead. "No."

I sighed. "That's what I figured."

I spent the rest of the drive back mentally preparing myself for how Marco might react. Based on the expression on Sal's face, I would have been better to spend my time figuring out where I was going to run for cover.

ELISABETH GRACE

CHAPTER TWENTY-SEVEN

I felt like a woman on a Death Row march as I trudged down the hallway toward the suite. Sal used his card to open the door, and I inhaled a deep breath before walking inside. I let it out as soon I heard Daniel and Leroy's laughter. Marco was nowhere to be found.

"Has Marco not returned yet?" Sal asked.

Leroy spun around in his position on the couch. "Haven't seen him since you guys left. How'd it go?"

Sal didn't bother answering. "I'm going to go find him." Without another word, he turned and headed right back out the door.

"Did you get your schoolwork done, buddy?" I asked with a smile, trying to lighten the mood.

"Well..." Daniel started.

"I might 'a distracted him before he was done. Don't give the boy trouble, that's on me," Leroy said.

I laughed. Daniel being behind on his school work

didn't seem like a huge offense in light of the fear that had gripped me half an hour ago.

"That's okay, Leroy." I turned my attention to my son. "Why don't you head over there and keep plugging away on it though."

"Okay, Mom." When he moved his wheelchair over toward the dining table, it made a noise I'd never heard before, like a high-pitched whining noise or something.

"Daniel, how long has your chair been making that sound?"

"That's the first I've heard it."

I pressed my lips together. "Okay, we'll keep an eye on it and see if it gets any worse. We might have to have it looked at."

The last thing I needed was for his chair to break down. It wasn't as if I could just go out and buy another one. Daniel's chair was custom-made especially for him, and he'd lose his independence without it.

Leroy gently led me to the hallway. "What's up, baby girl?"

I sighed. "There was an incident while we were out."

"What kind of incident?" His forehead wrinkled in obvious concern.

I relayed everything that had happened. When I was done, Leroy rubbed a hand over his bald head. "Sal's right, you know. Always trust your instincts."

"I know. I—"

The door to the suite swung open and Marco stalked in, fury evident in the tense lines of his face. His gaze immediately landed on me, but he blew right past me and headed in the direction of his room. "A word please?"

He'd used his manners, but there was nothing cordial

about the delivery. I felt like a child who'd done something wrong and was about to be punished.

"Thanks for staying with Daniel while I was out," I said to Leroy. "I'd better go deal with this."

He squeezed my shoulder. "Don't let him give you too much hell. That said, I do believe he really does have your best interests at heart."

"I know." My voice held the tone of a petulant child.

Leroy leaned in and gave me a hug. "I'm going to go find Sal so we can discuss what, if anything, we're going to do about what happened."

"Okay. See you later."

I turned in one direction and Leroy turned in the other. A part of me wished I could go with him, but I put my big girl panties on and headed to Marco's room.

I found him sitting on the end of the bed, bent over with his hands cradling his head. I mentally prepared myself to face his wrath.

No, I wasn't at fault for what had happened, but I'd seen Marco worked up before. He was more like a hurricane than a tornado, taking down everything in his path rather than picking and choosing what and who to destroy.

Tentatively, I stepped toward the bed. "Before you say anything—"

His head sprung up when he heard me and he reached out and yanked me to him, wrapping his arms around me and squeezing tight. We stayed like that for a while—me standing before him, his head pressed to my stomach, both of us clinging to one another.

I ran my fingers through his sweat-soaked hair. After several minutes, his grip on me loosened until he eventually pulled away, though he kept his hands on my hips as if I might try to escape.

"I was expecting Hurricane Marco," I said softly. He raised a brow. "Sometimes you're like a hurricane, decimating everything in your path. I'm not sure what *this* is."

He gave me a weak smile. "This is a man who is relieved that nothing happened to you."

It may have been *me* that was afraid for my life, but at that moment I felt the overwhelming need to comfort *him*.

I ran my fingers through the hair on one side of his head. "I'm starting to wonder if I just imagined the whole thing. Maybe I didn't even hear anything after all."

He shook his head. "You were right to run. Always trust this." He placed his hand low on my stomach. "It rarely leads you wrong."

"That's the same thing Sal said to me."

"And he's right." He waited a moment before continuing. "From now on, I don't want you going anywhere without me. Why were you at the building?"

I decided that we could argue over the me-not-going-anywhere-without-him comment some other time. "I don't want to tell you."

His head pulled back a bit, and he appeared affronted. "Why not?"

"You'll think it's stupid." I looked down at the floor.

Truth was, I was afraid he wouldn't take me seriously if I told him. Marco was a successful businessman. What would stop him from seeing me as a joke—the hooker with a heart who knew nothing about running a business?

"I assure you, I won't." He pulled me in close and set me on his lap. Apparently, the scent of dried sweat and cologne acted as an aphrodisiac because I wanted to squirm on his lap to relieve the tension.

"Someday I want to open a resource center for families of children with muscular dystrophy. I've been saving for a long time to try and make it happen. This building came on the market a while ago, and I wanted to see it."

Instead of laughing or looking skeptical, Marco leaned in and kissed the end of my nose. "You never fail to amaze me. I think it's a wonderful thing to do."

My jaw hung open for a moment before I recovered from my surprise. "You do?"

He nodded. "You know what these families are going through...how scared they are, the costs involved, what they really need help with. And it'd be a great way for Daniel to meet other children who are going through the same thing as him."

Tears pricked the corners of my eyes. So this was what it felt like when someone really believed in you.

"I take it back. You are a hurricane," I said softly.

Marco chuckled. "And why is that?"

"Because you just blew me right over with your response."

His face grew soft. "Tesoro…" He leaned in and our lips joined in a soothing kiss before he eventually pulled away.

"I tell you what. I have to fly to San Francisco in a few days for a business meeting. I was hoping you'd join me, and when we return, we can both go check out this building. Valenti Enterprises has developed a lot of land using existing buildings. Perhaps I can offer some insight or suggestions."

"I can't leave Daniel." Getting away from everything going on here sounded like heaven, but I couldn't leave my son behind.

"It's a quick trip. We'll leave on my plane mid-afternoon and return first thing the next morning. Leroy will be here, and we can ask Martina if she'll mind staying until breakfast. If you feel more comfortable, we can even ask Sal to stay behind, too."

"You have a plane?" I asked. My brain was stuck on that fact. He said it as if it wasn't a big deal, like everyone has their own private jet.

"My company does."

"What about us? Won't that put us in danger if Sal stays here?" I bit my lower lip. I couldn't believe I was even considering this.

"My contact there doesn't even know I'm coming yet, so there will be no time for them to plan anything ahead of time."

I mulled it over. This really wasn't all that different from me being absent for work until the middle of the night. I'd only be gone for a few extra hours, and most of that time Daniel would be sleeping anyway. The flight from Vegas to San Francisco wasn't a long one.

"And we'll come home *first* thing the next day?"

"First thing."

I remembered Daniel saying how I needed to have more fun and then recalled how wonderful the night out at the opera was. What would Marco have in store for us this time?

"Okay," I said simply.

"Really?" Marco's face beamed.

"Really."

He kissed me again, and suddenly the fear I felt earlier seemed so very distant—blown far away by Hurricane Marco.

CHAPTER TWENTY-EIGHT

The following day, Marco had the idea to take Daniel swimming in the hotel pool. So after he and Sal accompanied me to a quick appointment with one of Daniel's doctors, we ate lunch in the suite and then headed out.

It was a gorgeous day in early May, perfect for a day at the pool. Sal and Leroy would watch over us but remain out of sight so they didn't arouse Daniel's suspicion.

Because it was mid-week, the pool wasn't too packed. Most people soaked up the sun from their deck chairs, while a sprinkle of guests relaxed in the water.

This was my first time on the Bellagio's pool deck, and it didn't disappoint. There were two massive pools along with two smaller ones, each with a large fountain in the middle that reminded me of something you might see in a European town square. Oversized topiaries dotted the edges of the large pools, and the bright blue water looked refreshing as the surface rippled, distorting the pattern of the tiles beneath.

We picked a group of deck chairs near one of the large pools, and I set the bag I was carrying down while Marco rearranged the furniture so that there was room for Daniel to navigate his wheelchair in and out of the area. I loved that I didn't have to ask him to do it; he'd thought of it all on his own.

Daniel directed his chair over to the pool to check things out while I rummaged through my bag for some sunscreen. I'd applied Daniel's before we left the room, but I still needed to put some on myself. I pulled my cover-up off, revealing my black bikini, and tossed it on the chair.

When Marco was finished organizing the chairs to meet his OCD standards, he came up behind me and wrapped his arms around my waist. A small shiver broke out on my skin as his mouth pressed against my ear. "You'd better put that cover-up back on, otherwise all these people are going to get quite the show."

I playfully smacked his arm. "Behave, or Daniel will hear you," I whispered.

Marco nipped my ear. "We definitely don't want him to know what I want to do to his mother."

"Shhh," I scolded, laughing.

"Sure you don't need any help putting that sunscreen on?"

I rolled my eyes. "I think we'll be safer if you keep your distance."

He laughed and swatted my ass before he walked over to where Daniel had parked his wheelchair near the edge of the pool.

"Big enough for you?" Marco asked.

"It'll do," Daniel said in a joking way.

Marco chuckled. "Ready to go in?"

"Let's go!"

"All right." Marco ruffled Daniel's hair, and I'm pretty sure my ovaries would've sighed had they been able. "Let me ditch these clothes and we'll head in."

Marco turned and walked toward me, doing that sexy thing where guys reach behind their head and lift their shirt off. I still hadn't gotten used to how phenomenal his body was. Every time his chest was revealed to me, a rush of heat rocketed to my core.

The cocky bastard knew it too, if the smirk on his face was any indication. I'm sure my nipples poking out from underneath my bikini top didn't help conceal my desire either.

"You going to join us?" Marco asked. He pushed the athletic pants he was wearing down off his hips and let them drop to the ground.

My heartbeat picked up pace as I surveyed Marco's body. He wore a white Speedo, and all the muscles in his legs, arms, and abdomen flexed as he bent over to grab his pants and put them on the chair.

I'd never considered myself a fan of Speedos, but Marco had the body of a Greek god, and the white of his swimsuit highlighted his olive skin. There was nothing emasculating at all about how he wore the small amount of fabric. In fact, the Speedo only showcased exactly how *much* of a man Marco was. The prominent bulge beneath the material made my mouth water.

Here's hoping that thing was triple layered or he'd be showing everyone his assets. Selfishly, I sort of hoped it wasn't. I smiled to myself as I pictured what that would look like.

"Hey," he said and waved his hand in front of his

face. "You joining us?"

"Oh, yeah." I shook my head to break the sexual daze I'd fallen into. "As soon as I put my sunscreen on."

"See you in the water," he said, then leaned in to give me a quick peck on the mouth.

"I'll bring in Daniel's life jacket so he doesn't have to hold onto you the whole time."

He nodded and made his way back to the pool. I began to apply my sunscreen, the scent of coconut drifting into my nose as I spread the lotion over my skin.

I watched as Marco expertly lifted Daniel from his chair with one arm under his knees and one under his armpits, as if he'd done it a thousand times before. He carried him over to the steps and walked him into the water. Then he allowed Daniel to float on his back while he supported my son's frail body with his hands.

I let the feeling of contentment set into my bones as I enjoyed the scene in front of me. This was something that I'd remember for a long time.

A guy walking between deck chairs on the other side of the pool caught my eye, mostly because he was fully clothed and not dressed for the pool. His back was to me, but there was still something familiar about him. I felt sure I'd seen him before, but I shrugged it off since the man went back into the hotel and didn't seem to pay us any attention.

When I was fully protected from the sun, I joined Daniel and Marco in the pool. The water was cooler than the air, and it felt refreshing as it climbed further up my legs with each step down the stairs.

The boys were still in the same position as earlier, except Marco had his chin tipped down to look at Daniel. "Okay, try them all one more time."

Daniel noticed me approaching and called out to me. "Hey Mom, listen. Marco's teaching me how to describe people in Italian."

"I'm starting to think you're obsessed, buddy." Daniel was forever harassing Marco to teach him new words in Italian, and so far, Marco had been nice enough to indulge him whenever he asked.

"He is doing very well," Marco said with a proud smile.

"All right. Let's hear it." I began to tread water beside them.

"Capelli castani, rossi, biondi, neri, grigi."

"Perfecto," Marco said, beaming.

Daniel grinned back at him and then turned his attention toward me. "That's all the colors of people's hair, Mom."

"I'm impressed. You're doing so good."

"He really is," Marco said. "He has a natural talent for it."

"Maybe I could be a translator or something when I grow up," Daniel said.

A small smile formed on my face. "You can be anything you want to be, buddy."

The far-off future wasn't something I thought a lot about. There were so many ways Daniel's disorder could prevent him from reaching adulthood that I tried not to think that far ahead.

When he was a little baby, I used to obsess over it to the point that I nearly drove myself mad. I couldn't enjoy any of our moments together because I was always worried about what might happen down the road. Once I realized that, I promised myself that I'd focus on the time we *did* have together and not worry about what *might* happen. Growing up, my mom used to say, *'Don't borrow trouble.'* Where my son was concerned, it was how I lived my life.

"Do you want to put your life jacket on so you can float around on your own for a bit?" I asked Daniel.

"Okay."

Marco held him above the water so I could fit his life jacket on him.

Laughter erupted from a group of teenagers who'd obviously been abandoned by their parents in favor of the casino. They were huddled on a group of deck chairs at the far side of the pool. I wasn't able to make out exactly what they were saying, but I caught the words 'freak' and 'problem.' It was obvious from their less than furtive glances that they were talking about us.

My cheeks heated in anger. Why did people have to be so cruel to someone just because they were different from them?

I noticed Marco's gaze flick over in their direction a couple of times, but Daniel seemed blessedly oblivious as he rattled on about an ad for a video game that he'd seen on television.

"So can we get it, Mom?"

"Pardon?" I asked while I fastened the final buckle on the life jacket.

"The game, can I get it?"

"I don't think so. You know how I feel about those things."

His bottom lip pushed out and he sulked for a minute, but Marco picked him up and pretended he was going to dunk him in the water. His pout quickly turned into laughter.

We all horsed around for a while, and it was clear that Daniel was enjoying himself. He'd done some water therapy in the past to help maintain the strength in his muscles, but it was rare that he got to play in a pool the same way other kids his age did.

After half an hour or so, Marco announced that he was off to use the restroom. I thought nothing of it until I noticed him heading toward the group of kids that had been eyeing us earlier. They'd continued to blatantly stare at us while we'd been playing around in the water.

My stomach rolled, hoping that he wasn't going to make a scene. I turned Daniel so his back was to the group and continued to play with him while keeping an eye on what was unfolding on the other side of the pool deck.

It was clear Marco wasn't pleased. His finger pointed from one person to the other as he spoke, and the tension in the muscles of his back was evident.

I was out of earshot so I couldn't hear what he was saying, but the crowd around him didn't appear to be putting up much of a fight. One of the guys looked like he might be thinking of arguing with Marco, but the rest nodded their heads, looking somewhat contrite. Marco said something else to them before turning back around and returning to the pool.

My eyes were wide as he dove off the end of the stairs and swam over to us underwater. He rose up beside me and shook out his hair, splashing the two of us. We laughed and Marco slicked his hair back with his hands.

"Everything okay?" I asked hesitantly, my gaze darting over to the group.

"It is now." He nodded and turned his attention to Daniel.

"What do you think of me taking your mom away on a special trip for the night?" Marco asked him.

I'd mentioned the trip to Daniel earlier that morning and he'd seemed okay with it, but I still questioned whether or not it was the right thing to do.

"It's awesome!" Daniel said. "I get to have a sleepover with Martina, and she said she's going to let me put extra whipped cream on my pancakes in the morning if I want."

I laughed and splashed a little water at him. "Oh, she did, did she?"

"Yep. And I'm going to see if she'll put double the amount of chocolate chips, too."

"So I guess you won't miss me at all, huh?" I asked, winking at him.

"Nah," he said, kicking as best he was able and floating a little farther away from us. "You're not even going to be gone for a whole day."

Marco and I both laughed. "Tell me how you really feel, buddy," I said.

"All right," Marco said. "What do you say we play a game of Marco Polo?"

"Really, *Marco*?" I chuckled.

"What, are you scared because I'm obviously going to win *my* game? I was thinking boys on one team—"

"Me on the other?" I raised a brow.

"Yeah!" Daniel cheered.

I looked between the two of them and crossed my arms in front of me. "Bring it."

Marco's gaze dipped down to my chest. "Oh, I will. You just wait."

He lived up to his promise that night...several times.

CHAPTER TWENTY-NINE

The only reason I was able to step on the plane was because I didn't want to disappoint Daniel. He'd been so excited for me—and I think a little for himself—that when I started second-guessing my decision to head to San Francisco, I kept moving one foot in front of the other, remembering the gleam in his eyes.

I'd never been away from him for so long, and though it was only a handful of hours more than usual, I think he was thrilled to have a little independence. I was learning that nine-year-old boys, whether they had muscular dystrophy or not, liked their freedom every once and a while.

"Would you like to join me at my meeting or stay here?" Marco asked.

We'd arrived at the hotel and were unpacking our things. The room was lovely with white furnishings and a mix of cream and champagne fabrics used throughout. The carpet was so lush that your feet sunk into it.

"I have no business being at your meeting, Marco. I'll stay here."

He stepped toward me and tucked a piece of hair behind my ear. "I don't know about that. I'm sure you could teach everyone a thing or two."

I laughed. "I appreciate your confidence, but I think I'll leave this one to you."

"Very well. Why don't you relax and get ready for dinner? We can leave when I return." He leaned down and kissed the top of my head.

"Okay," I said softly.

"Don't open the door for anyone, you understand? We are far from Vito's reach, but that doesn't mean I want some strange person in here with you while you're alone."

A chill radiated from my spine at the reminder of Vito. I nodded my head in agreement.

"I shouldn't be more than a couple of hours, and then we'll have some fun."

"Take care of what you need to. Don't worry about me." I smiled.

"I always worry about you, cara." He gave me a proper kiss this time that made my toes curl inside my shoes. I reluctantly let him pull away. "I'd better go before we end up spending all of our time in San Francisco in this hotel room."

After seeing him out, I fastened the deadbolt and slid the chain lock in place. Then I glanced around the silent and empty hotel room.

Relax. *Right.*

The truth was, I hadn't been by myself since...well, it had to have been before Daniel was born.

I thought about a soak in the large tub, but I was

really hoping to include Marco in that activity at some point during our stay. I switched on the television just to fill the room with some noise so that I didn't feel so alone and out of sorts.

There were many times while raising my son that I'd wished for even a moment or two of solitude. Now that I had it, I found it felt unnatural and wasn't nearly as much fun as I thought it would be.

I figured that since I couldn't relax, I might as well get some of my coursework done. Good thing I brought my laptop.

An hour passed and I was feeling accomplished. Since I had a few minutes before I needed to start getting ready for dinner, I decided to call Martina to see how things were going there.

It rang twice before she picked up. "Hello."

"Hey, Martina. It's me. How are things going on your end?"

"Fine, fine." She laughed.

"What's so funny?" I asked.

"Daniel said you'd call."

I rolled my eyes, though neither of them could see it. "He did, did he?"

"Oh yes. He said you wouldn't be able to help yourself."

I chuckled. "Well, he knows his mother, that's for sure."

"Don't you worry yourself. We're just fine."

"I know." I sighed. "You know it has nothing to do with me not trusting you, right?"

"Of course I do. This is a big step for you."

"It is. Can you believe that I have a couple of hours

to myself and have no idea what to do?"

Martina's laughter echoed through the receiver. "Ah, a mother's curse."

"I guess so."

"There is one thing I wanted to mention," she said with a note of concern in her voice. "That sound coming from Daniel's chair is getting worse. It's much louder now."

Shit. "Does it still work?"

"Yes, it seems to still move fine."

"Okay. Thanks for the heads-up. I'm going to call the guy that does the maintenance on it and see if he can squeeze us in tomorrow before it breaks."

"Sounds good. Do you want to talk to Daniel before you go?"

"Yes, please. Thanks for your help, Martina."

"No thanks necessary. You know I love that boy like he's my own."

A lump formed in my throat. To the outside world, it probably didn't seem like I'd received many blessings, but that was completely untrue. My son may have his challenges, but he was surrounded by a small number of people who truly cared for his well-being. For that I considered myself extremely blessed.

"Hey, Mom."

Daniel's voice instantly eased the tension I hadn't realized I'd been carrying with me since we left.

"Hey buddy, how are you doing?"

"Good."

"So you knew I'd call, did you?" I laughed.

"Kinda. I figured you would anyway. You always worry so much."

"Like I keep telling you, it's my job."

"I know, I know."

I smiled. "Okay, well have fun and I'll see you in the morning. Is there anything you want me to bring back for you?"

He paused as if he were thinking about it for a moment, if the silence on the other end was any indication. "Nah. You and Marco just have fun. That'll make me the most happy."

I sniffed back tears. My son was so thoughtful and caring. "Okay, buddy. I promise I'll do that. See you tomorrow. I love you."

"I love you, too, Mom. See ya."

The line went dead, but I sat there staring at the phone for a few minutes in wonder. *God, they grow up so fast.*

Shaking off the bit of melancholy that came with that realization, I vowed to do exactly as Daniel had requested and enjoy my evening with Marco.

A knock sounded at the door, and I peered through the peephole to see Marco standing there. I removed the chain lock, unlocked the deadbolt, and swung the door wide open with a smile.

I'd already showered, put on my make-up, gotten dressed, and fixed my hair. I had decided to wear my hair down with beach waves and wore a black bodycon dress paired with silver stilettos.

"Bella doesn't even do you justice." His gaze wandered from head to toe and back again before he stepped into the room, wrapped his arms around me, and kicked the door shut behind him. "Though I'm beginning to wish we didn't have reservations." He squeezed my ass in his hands. "Give me a couple of minutes to freshen up and then we can leave."

"Sounds good." I resisted the urge to run my hands all over his hard body, knowing if I started we'd probably never see the inside of the restaurant. I'd never been to San Francisco before, and I wanted to see more than just the hotel room.

Twenty minutes later the car service deposited us in front of a building near Fisherman's Wharf. The restaurant had a charming, white stucco exterior. Twilight was approaching and the inside of the building glowed from the soft lighting, creating a warm and inviting atmosphere.

Once the hostess had seated us and we'd placed our orders with the waiter, I relaxed into my seat with my glass of wine. "How did your meeting go?"

Marco shrugged. "They were surprised to see me, which was what I was hoping for." I raised my eyebrows in question. "The company I went to see supplies our properties in Europe with the little shampoo and conditioner bottles you see in hotel rooms, as well as soaps and other amenities." I nodded, knowing what he meant. "We've had consistency issues with the quality of some of the products, not to mention shipping delays and them sending the wrong product. It sounds like a small thing, but Valenti Enterprises has only high-end properties, servicing a very specific type of clientele. Providing them with inferior products, or worse, having to tell them that we can't provide them at all during their stay is not acceptable."

I swallowed a sip of my wine and placed the glass back on the table. "Were you able to resolve the issue?"

"I was able to get to the bottom of the issue. In time, it will be resolved." Marco picked up the glass in front of him and took a sip before continuing. "It seems the father who ran the company has fallen ill and his daughter has stepped in to fill his role over the past year. It has been...challenging for her."

"Why didn't they say anything to you?"

"He and my father had a good relationship, but they were reluctant to because they thought that I'd pull the business."

"Do you plan to?"

He shook his head. "No. Now that I know the problem, I can work with them. We have a longstanding relationship with this company, and I know first-hand the challenge of stepping in to fill someone else's shoes. I made it clear that we wouldn't accept inferior products, but there are things we can do on our end to help. I'll make sure procurement gives longer lead times when ordering. They were afraid to miss their delivery dates, so if they were missing an ingredient and the lead time to receive it was too far away, they'd use a cheaper substitute. But that impacts quality. Longer lead times will allow them to better plan ahead until they've worked out the kinks—or the father comes back to the business, whichever comes first."

Marco was a businessman with a heart. I admired that instead of cutting ties in the face of adversity, he went the extra mile to help.

"That's very admirable of you. I'm sure a lot of people would've just made a phone call and ended the relationship." I twirled my wine glass on the table.

"Sometimes you need a face-to-face meeting to get to the bottom of the problem. After all, business is all about relationships. You need to trust the people you're in business with. Without trust, you cannot depend on one another."

I gazed across the table at this fascinating man who

was so full of contradictions. How did I get so lucky? He could probably have any woman he wanted, yet here I sat, the object of his affection. "You're a good man, Marco."

He smiled, but it didn't reach his eyes. In fact, he looked a little melancholy to me. "Even the angel has a devil that sits on his shoulder."

"What does that mean?" I asked and took another sip of wine.

He reached across the table and placed his hand on mine. "Even good people have bad in them. I am like any other man. The opportunity to be evil—greedy, stubborn, egotistical, narcissistic—it's all there. I just choose not to feed that particular beast."

I crinkled my forehead. "Why do you always do that?"

"Do what?" Marco released my hand and brought his tumbler to his mouth for a drink. "Whenever I pay you a compliment, you immediately turn it around and imply that you're not a good person, when everything I've seen indicates differently."

He smiled again, but this time there was life in his eyes. "You make me want to be an even better person than I was already trying to be."

"You're avoiding the question." I crossed my arms over my chest.

"And *you're* very perceptive." When I didn't speak, budge, or breathe, he sighed. "I'm not a perfect man, nor am I an innocent one. I never want to lie to you by making you think otherwise."

I relaxed my stance and leaned back against my chair. "I don't think you're perfect. But being perfect doesn't make someone a good person, Marco. Their actions and intentions do." I shrugged. "That's what I believe anyway."

"Then you must believe yourself to be a good person." The corners of his full lips tilted up to form a small smile.

"Why?" I took another sip of my wine.

"Why?" He leaned forward in his chair. "Is it not you who told me a few days ago that you've been saving your money for years so that you could open a center to help those with muscular dystrophy?"

Heat rose to my cheeks. "That doesn't mean anything. I'm sure your company donates to all kinds of charities." I wasn't comfortable being painted as a saint.

"Yes, Valenti Enterprises throws money at a bunch of charities. But neither myself nor my employees are in the trenches dealing with those who need the help. That's what you want to do. Put yourself in the trenches."

I wasn't sure what to say. I'd never thought of it that way. "I guess," I reluctantly agreed.

"Tell me about your vision for this place. If money was no object and everything could be just as you want it...what would it look like?"

I felt a little silly talking about this with a millionaire—or billionaire, for all I knew—when here I was trying to scrape together the funds just to put a down payment on the place. But he appeared genuinely interested, so I responded.

"Well, I'd put a fresh coat of white paint on the building and probably paint the accents green. Not a dark green like an evergreen, but a lighter green. Something fresh and hopeful. There'd be a reception area when you walk in with lots of chairs to sit, but there'd be plenty of room beside them to fit wheelchairs. The entire building would be handicap accessible, of course. We'd offer support to families whose children have the disorder—medical, mental, and financial. Since a good portion of the children with MD end up being home-schooled, I'd like to have a classroom at the center where they can all gather every day and do their lessons. That way they're not missing out on the camaraderie of having classmates. We'd have physical therapists on-site, breathing specialists, and obviously a doctor. I also think it'd be wonderful to offer the families social outings that we can all do together." I looked down at my lap, embarrassed that I'd gone on and on. "Sorry, I'm rambling."

"Not at all." His eyes held a touch of wonder as he watched me from across the table. "But I can tell that you've given this a lot of thought."

I laughed. "I've had years to daydream about it."

"May I propose a toast then?" Marco reached for his tumbler and raised it into the air, and I followed suit with my wine glass.

"To making your dream happen. To helping these families and these children live the best lives they can."

There was so much confidence in his voice that he almost had me believing that somehow I'd really make it happen.

CHAPTER THIRTY

The rest of dinner was spent getting to know one another better, and since we had an early flight in the morning, Marco insisted that we return to our hotel room right afterward.

He passed me the key card as we approached our room, which I found a little odd but I didn't question it. I took the key from him and inserted it into the door. When the little light turned green, I pushed down on the handle and swung the door open.

"Oh my God." I gasped, and my hand flew up to cover my mouth.

The room was lit with what had to be close to a hundred candles. A pleasant vanilla scent filled the suite, and the effect created a cozy, cave-like feeling as the golden flames flickered and bounced soft light off the pale walls. Classical music played in the background, and as I stepped further into the room, I realized the bathroom was lit with candles, too.

"How did you manage this?" I turned around in circles so that I didn't miss a thing.

Marco came to me, one hand cupping the back of my neck and the other my face. His thumb softly grazed the skin of my cheek as he gazed down at me. "A few well placed phone calls." He grinned.

"It's so romantic. Thank you." I perched up on my toes and brought my lips to his. Our kiss was slow and sensual, and we took our time tasting each other until Marco pulled away.

"There should be a hot bath drawn. Why don't we slip into the tub before the water gets cold?"

I nodded, not wanting to say a word and ruin this intimate moment.

I walked to the bathroom with Marco behind me and stopped, motioning to the zipper on the back of my dress. He took the hint and pulled my zipper down inch by inch until the fabric fell to the floor. I wore no bra, and when I turned to face him, his pupils dilated as his gaze slipped from my breasts down to my lace thong and finally to the heels I still wore.

I pushed his suit jacket off his shoulders and he let it fall to the ground. While I worked on unbuttoning his shirt, Marco removed his tie and untucked the bottom of his shirt before he slipped it off entirely.

He leaned down to kiss me again, and my nipples tightened further when they met the soft skin of his hard chest. Marco's hands skimmed down my back and cupped my ass, pushing me against his arousal. I moaned into his mouth and he pulled away.

"Easy, dolcezza. I have plans for us this evening. If

we keep going, it will be over before I've even started with you."

Heat pooled in the center of my thighs at his promise of things to come.

Marco's thumbs slipped beneath the lace at either side of my underwear and dragged them down my thighs until he was on his knees before me. I steadied myself on his shoulders and pulled one foot out, then the other.

His heavy-lidded dark eyes gazed up at me from below, and I pushed my fingers through his hair. He leaned in to the apex of my thighs and inhaled deeply. There was something so deeply erotic about what he'd done that my knees almost buckled.

"I can't wait to taste you later." His voice was raspy. Marco stood to his full height again, and I immediately went to work to shed the rest of his clothes.

When we were both completely exposed, we did nothing but gaze upon each other. Several moments passed before I reached out and ran my hand down his muscled chest, feeling each and every dip and hard edge beneath my fingertips and committing each one to memory.

Marco palmed my breast, lightly dragging his thumb over my nipple until it was so erect it was almost painful.

"Let me help you into the water," he said.

I took his hand and dipped my foot into the bubbles in the oversized tub. The water was the perfect temperature and seemed to wrap itself around my foot like a satin glove.

Once I was seated, Marco slipped in behind me and then pulled me closer to him so that my back was to his chest as I sat between his legs. His hardness pressed into my lower back, but we were both content to soak in the warm water and relax into each other.

His hands caressed my shoulders and then ran down the length of my arms and back up again. My breathing picked up when his hands moved down to my hips before dipping between my legs. He didn't touch my core but simply ran his fingers along the inside of my thighs, back up my stomach, and over my breasts. He repeated this motion several times. It was relaxing, and yet it heightened my nerve endings at every point of contact where his fingers traced over my skin.

Eventually the water grew tepid, and we were forced to leave the cocoon of intimacy we'd created. Marco climbed out first and then helped me out, drying off my skin with one of the plush hotel towels. Once we were no longer wet, he took my hand and led me back out to the bedroom, where he walked over to the nightstand and grabbed something off the corner.

It was a black lace blindfold. The vision of a naked Marco holding that thing and walking toward me had me practically panting in anticipation.

When he reached me, Marco held the blindfold between us. "Do you trust me?"

I bit my bottom lip and nodded. One corner of Marco's lip tipped up before he covered my eyes with the fabric.

If I really wanted to see, I could make out basic shapes through the thick lace but no real details. I realized that wasn't the point though. This was about trust and denying me one of my senses.

I closed my eyes and was surrounded by darkness. I could hear Marco's breathing so I knew he was still nearby. The scent of the vanilla candles filling the room seemed stronger now that my brain was no longer working to process the images I was seeing.

"Have you ever heard of Tantra?" his low voice rumbled in my ear.

"Kind of."

Something soft dragged along my back from one shoulder to the next. *A feather, maybe?*

"I first heard of this when I traveled to India on business many years ago. The idea intrigued me, so I read many books about it. I've never had anyone to practice it with. Until now."

The feather caressed the skin from the top of my spine all the way down, one slow inch at a time, until it reached the crest of my ass.

"Tantra is about the connection of the mind and spirit, not just our bodies." Marco's voice moved from behind me around to the front.

He circled my nipple with the feather. The sensation was enough to arouse me, but too light to provide any relief. I let out a small moan, wanting him to soothe me, to provide me with some reprieve.

He didn't. Instead, he circled the other nipple before trailing the feather down the center of my chest, past my belly button, and over my mound.

I let my head fall back as a small sweat broke out over my skin. Marco hadn't said as much, but I instinctively knew I wasn't to reach out for him. This experience was about the build-up—and building something more intimate between us.

The feather continued down the inside of my thigh and toward my calf. He must be on his knees in front of me now. Once he reached my ankle, the soft caress of the feather swept over my foot and then was gone.

He left me like that for a minute while I stood there,

naked and wanting. The only sound in the room was the classical music playing softly in the background.

His hand lightly gripped my calf before the feeling of something rough being dragged along the outside of my leg caused an entirely different sensation to race through my body.

I had no guess what this item might be, but it scratched me as it moved over my heated skin—not in an unpleasant way, just in a way that had me consumed with lust. I wasn't sure whether I wanted to beg for more or plead for him to stop.

When he reached the top of my thigh, he slid the item over my mound again. I cried out a little.

My clit throbbed in anticipation, and I was pretty close to begging him to touch me there—*really* touch me there.

The rough points of the undistinguishable object dragged across my breast, eventually connecting with my nipple. It was too much for me.

My head snapped back up. "Marco, please," I begged.

"Shh," he whispered in my ear. He was behind me now. "You and I are going to bring each other to the edge so many times tonight. We won't find relief until we're truly joined as one on every level. It will be both heaven and hell." He pressed his hot, naked flesh into mine from behind, his arousal prominent as it dug into my back. "You will curse my name like the devil and then scream it out like a benediction."

"Oh, God," I whispered.

His deep chuckle sounded in my ear. "You may want to call me that when we're done, yes."

"Cocky bastard," I said.

"Let's get you onto the bed," he said, already leading

me there by my arm. "Then I can show you exactly why that is."

I gulped as Marco spun me and pressed a little on my shoulders. As I sunk down, I put my arms out behind me until I felt the mattress beneath my palms. Then I let my weight fall fully until I was seated on the edge of the bed.

Marco pulled the blindfold off my face, and I blinked a couple of times so that my eyes could adjust to the orange glow of the candlelit room.

Marco stood over me, the flames of the flickering candles reflecting off his dark eyes. In that moment, he looked every bit the part of a fallen angel.

"Lay down on the bed," he commanded in a raspy voice. We might have been trying something different here tonight, but pieces of the man I knew—the domineering and commanding one—still showed themselves.

I scooted back so that I lay in the middle of the bed.

He walked alongside the bed toward the nightstand, his hard as steel erection bobbing with every step. My mouth watered and I licked my lips, wishing I could taste him right now. Reaching down, he opened the top drawer and pulled out what appeared to be a small bottle of massage oil. My skin instantly tingled as I envisioned all the things he could do to me.

"Turn over," he said. His voice was soft, but it sounded like a command anyway.

I did as he asked and rolled over so I was lying on my stomach, my arms stretched out over the top of my head. I felt his weight shift the mattress as he made his way closer to me. The oil hit my back seconds before one of his large hands started to massage it into my skin. He coated much of my back with the slippery liquid, and then I heard the lid click closed and felt the bottle drop onto the mattress.

Before I knew it, he'd straddled me so that he was sitting on my thighs and his hands worked the oil along my skin. He wasn't massaging me, at least not in the traditional sense. He was simply running his palms flat along the length of my back and over my ass cheeks, but not digging his fingers into my flesh.

The delicious friction felt equal parts erotic and relaxing, and though my sex was on fire for this man, I couldn't seem to muster the willpower to wiggle out from under him and tell him to stop so we could get to the part where he was sinking inside of me.

He continued for several minutes before telling me to turn over again. I did as he asked. This time, instead of sitting on top of my legs, he sat so that his legs were spread around me, my own were spread and draped over him, hanging off to the side. If I'd made a circle with my limbs, I'd be wrapped around his waist.

The length of his arousal pressed against my core, and I could barely stop myself from writhing against him to get the friction I was so desperately looking for. The only thing stopping me was the expression on his face as he gazed down at me. It was one of adoration and awe, and I could've looked at it all night. Especially because it was directed at me.

Marco reached for the bottle of massage oil and held it over me. He drizzled it all over my chest before making a line down the middle of my stomach, over my belly button, and finally reaching my mound. He let the oil soak into the very few curls I had there before he capped the bottle again and tossed it aside.

Both his hands reached down for me, but instead of spreading the massage oil as I'd imagined he'd do, he ran his hands up and down the length of my body without actually touching me. He was only millimeters above my skin, but the energy in his hands still affected me, causing my skin to tingle. Within a minute I was moaning, not so silently begging him to touch me.

It was as if we were both magnets—every one of my nerve endings pulled to him by some unseen force when his hands passed over me.

When I could take no more and my entire body was fraught with tension and need, he lowered his large hands down onto my skin.

The relief was swift. I exhaled the first full breath I'd taken in the last several minutes. His expert hands performed the same type of massage he did on my back, only this time he was working with more sensitive areas. When his palms crested the top of my breasts and rubbed against my nipples, I had to bite the inside of my cheek to keep from crying out.

He noticed. "Let it out, amore mio. I want to be able to read your body so that I can take you places you've only dreamed about."

His hands slid over my mound and I cried out, mostly because he didn't touch me where I desperately needed him to. Instead, he used his hands to massage my outer lips. I was panting hard now, trying to control the urge that made me want to use my own hand for some sweet relief.

Marco must have sensed that I was on the edge, because in the next moment his thumb and index finger slowly entered my inner lips and he moved them up and down the length of my sex.

I sighed in relief. It was enough to make me feel like I wasn't going to go crazy at least. His fingers traced over my slit without entering and then gently stroked my clitoris. They moved in a clockwise motion, then counter-clockwise, always changing the direction, the rhythm, and the motion so I was worked up as hell, but couldn't get myself to a place where I could finish.

The air in the room was warm from all of the candles, and between that and the orange glow cast across every surface, I felt cocooned in a blissful state and I never wanted it to end.

Marco pressed the heel of his hand to my clit, rapidly moving it back and forth. The vibration lit up every nerve ending in my core, and he maintained eye contact with me as he worked me into a fervor. The intimacy of this moment was something I'd never experienced before. It was unsettling and overwhelming and scary as hell. More than that though, it felt right and necessary and inevitable.

He slowly pressed his fingers into me with his other hand and curled them so they were pressed against my G-spot. It wasn't long before I was barreling toward an orgasm, but instead of finishing me off, Marco slowed his rhythm and gently led me away from the edge.

Then he slowly worked me back up again, his heavy-lidded gaze taking in my every response, before bringing me back down. He did this so many times that my entire body was trembling. I was *so* close to coming.

I pleaded with him and a warm smile formed on his face. When he removed his hands from my body, I immediately missed our connection.

Marco crossed his legs in front of him, and with the two fingers he just had inside me, he motioned me over to him. "Come here."

As I drew near, he placed his hands on my waist and pulled me toward him. I was sitting on his lap with my legs wrapped around him and our chests touching as we embraced one another.

"This is the Yab Yum position," he said.

We sat together like that, feeling our connection as if it were a living, breathing thing between us. Eventually our breathing unified as if we'd become one being, not two separate people. I'd bet that even our heartbeats were in sync.

As Marco stared at me with love in his eyes, the immense urge to weep overpowered me, filling me like a vessel. The joy I felt in that moment was so intense that it was difficult to control my reaction. Sometimes there was just so much happiness inside you that it was impossible for it not to spill over and out of you.

"I need you to know something," Marco said in a low, raspy voice. My breath hitched, knowing that there would be no going back from whatever he was going to say in these next moments. "I see you for who you *really* are. I don't look at you and see what you do to make money. I see the woman, the mother, the lover, the friend."

My breathing sputtered a bit as I took in his words— words that acted as a salve to my bruised and battered soul.

His dark eyes drank me in and he continued. "You need to know that I am in love with you. Deep, soul-shattering, no-coming-back-from it love that I cannot keep to myself any longer."

Tears of joy sprung to my eyes because I could feel the love he spoke of. I felt it envelop me, sink in through my pores, and spread out inside of me until every single cell in my body was ready to burst.

"I love you, too," I whispered. It was the first time I'd admitted the truth—to myself even—but it was freeing. And honest. And right.

Our mouths joined, but rather than a fevered kiss, we slowly explored one another as if we had all the time in the world. The pull I felt toward Marco on an average day had always astounded me, but in that perfect moment, I don't think I could have separated from him if my life depended on it. We were two bodies, but we were united in spirit. Our souls were now so tangled up in each other that there was no telling one from the other.

Marco rose to a kneeling position and sat back on his heels. I unraveled my legs from around him and placed my knees on the mattress on either side of him. His hands cupped my ass and drew me up before I sank down on top of him, never letting my eyes leave his.

I rode him up and down, swiveling my hips when he was fully seated inside of me until we were both ready to climax. Then I slowed my rhythm, taking my cue from him earlier.

His hard length filled me and he set a steady, bone-melting pace. My clit was engorged and throbbing, yet my breathing was somehow slow and labored.

As I took him inside of me over and over again, the love that I had for this complicated man overwhelmed me, and I wanted to give him something in return for all he'd given me. Something that would prove that I'd handed over my entire heart and soul to him.

"Emily," I whispered. Recognition lit his eyes, followed swiftly by gratification. He knew the significance of what I'd given him. "My real name is Emily Ross."

He kissed me with more passion than I'd ever felt before and pushed up into me from below. My impending orgasm was a runaway train barreling down the tracks and picking up speed. I knew that this time there would be no holding off.

He moved into me as I moved into him, and neither of us looked away from the other for a second. I fell apart gazing into his eyes and he followed me into bliss. White light surrounded me as the room disappeared, and for one perfect moment I was overcome with love and rapture and joy.

When I came to, Marco was still pulsing inside of me, moaning as the final piece of him poured into me. We brought our foreheads to rest against each other, trying to control our breathing. I was clutching him and he was doing the same to me.

"Thank you," he whispered.

I laughed a little. "For the orgasm?" I joked, still catching my breath.

He shook his head. "No. For giving me you. *All* of you." We melted into a kiss, our sweat-soaked skin, mine covered with massage oil, making us stick together.

"Emily is a beautiful name for a beautiful woman."

I knew this night had changed everything and there would be no going back. I knew I couldn't willingly give my body to another man after this. I knew I had to figure it all out.

But in the aftermath of our lovemaking, I was satisfied to push all of that away because I finally knew what it meant to be in love with someone.

It was a sacrifice and an honor that you bestowed upon someone when you trusted them enough to give them the only thing that truly had the power to destroy you.

Your love.

There was nothing in the world more fulfilling *or* more terrifying.

CHAPTER THIRTY-ONE

The next morning Marco and I enjoyed an early breakfast together in the hotel's restaurant before heading to the airport. I was anxious to see Daniel, so we'd decided that Leroy would drive him and Martina to meet us at the airport when we landed in Vegas.

Daniel had been so excited when we'd told him. Forget the fact that it was a private airfield; he'd never even seen a plane up close before.

The pilot was preparing for take-off and I'd just buckled my seatbelt when Marco took my hand and threaded his fingers through mine. He brought my hand to his lips and gently kissed the back of it.

"Last night was perfect," he said.

"It was," I agreed. I brought my free hand to his cheek.

"I meant every word I said, Emily." My breath caught in my throat. I still wasn't used to hearing my real name on his lips.

He leaned in and kissed me slowly and with purpose. "I love you, and there is nothing I wouldn't do to protect you and make you happy."

"I know," I said softly. With my head and my whole heart, I believed him, and more than that, I felt the same way. I had no idea what that meant for the two of us—or my career, for that matter—but we'd work it out. There was no use denying what was so obvious to us both.

We belonged together.

I leaned my head against Marco's shoulder as the sound of the engines grew louder, signaling our imminent departure. I smiled to myself, thinking how funny it was that we were about to fly into the clouds when I was already on cloud nine for the first time in my life.

Less than two hours later, our private plane landed in Las Vegas.

"Time to return the princess to her castle," Marco said with his hand extended to help me out of my seat.

I laughed. "This princess is ready to return. It's not such a bad castle." I pushed up on my tiptoes and placed a chaste kiss on his lips.

Marco's arm wound around my back and pulled me in closer, deepening the kiss before he eventually pulled away. "We will have to do a trip like that again. Maybe wine country next time."

I smiled and a warm feeling filled my chest. "That sounds wonderful."

Marco released me and we said goodbye to the flight attendant and flight crew then made our way down the stairs onto the tarmac. Marco took my hand in his and together we walked toward Sal, who stood waiting by the car.

As we made our way across the asphalt, I really did feel like a princess. And it was all thanks to Marco. *Was this really my life?*

We were both smiling, thrilled with our newfound love. Things were almost perfect. The only thing missing was—

Daniel.

Where was Leroy and the van? Where were Daniel and Martina?

Sal removed his sunglasses, and Marco was the first to know something was terribly wrong. I knew it because the minute Sal's gaze met his, Marco's hand squeezed mine to the point that it caused me pain.

My steps faltered and my stomach twisted.

"Che e' successo?" Marco asked.

"C'e' stato un incidente."

"Che tipo di incidente?"

"Il ragazzo e' stato rapito."

I looked at Marco to see what his response would be to whatever Sal just said. His face crumpled and he let my hand drop then shoved his hands through his hair.

I looked back and forth between the pair of men. "Would someone please tell me what's going on!" There was no mistaking the frantic tone to my voice.

Marco turned to me with tears in his eyes.

I took a couple steps back from him, my head frantically shaking while my stomach took a nosedive toward the center of the earth. "No," I whispered. "No."

My knees gave way and I fell toward the ground, but Marco grabbed me before I crashed. "He's alive, Emily."

I squeezed my eyes shut and the tears began to fall,

though they were so hot they felt like acid rolling along my skin. "What happened?" I croaked out.

Sal answered this time. "Daniel was kidnapped on the way here. They left early to make a stop at the pharmacy to pick up his medication."

My mind was spinning. I was barely able to form a complete or coherent thought, so much so that I wasn't able to connect the dots in that moment. "Who? Who would do this?" I screamed.

"Presumably Vito's men," Sal responded, his voice void of emotion. I collapsed into Marco.

"Emily, they won't hurt him. He's their collateral," Marco offered.

His words didn't make me feel any better. "This is all my fault. If I hadn't gone to San Francisco, maybe they would've taken me instead."

Marco squeezed me tighter. "This is not your fault."

"Yes, yes it is." I pushed my hands through my hair.

Oh God. What was I going to do? "What if they hurt him? My poor boy. He must be so scared!" My voice had become more and more shrill with every word I spoke.

Marco gave me a small shake. "Right now you need to be strong for your son so we can figure out how to get him back."

I sniffed back my tears. He was right. I didn't have time to fall apart right now, no matter how badly I wanted to.

"How do we get him back?" I looked from Marco to Sal. Sal to Marco. Neither seemed in a hurry to respond. "Well?" I yelled.

Marco placed his hand on my lower back and glanced around. "Let's get back to the suite and we'll discuss our options."

"Options?" Anger raced from my stomach up to my throat. "The only option is that we get Daniel back. Period."

"Of course that's the only option." He looked a little hurt that I'd thought he was implying differently, but I didn't have time to worry about that right now.

I ran ahead of him and crawled into the back of the SUV. Both men followed me, and within seconds the vehicle was speeding off the tarmac.

I chewed on my fingernails and rocked back and forth on the seat. I couldn't help picturing Daniel with the type of people who would kidnap an innocent child. Was he afraid? Crying? Was he calling out for me, wondering why I wasn't there breaking down the doors to get to him?

"Tell me what happened." I said it loud enough to know that Sal had heard me in the front seat. He exhaled a large breath.

"All I know is that they were on their way to the pharmacy and then headed here. Leroy said that another car bumped into the back of the van while they were waiting at a traffic light, so he got out to investigate. The next thing he remembers is him and Martina waking up in a parking lot in an industrial park outside of town."

My hand flew up to cover my mouth. I'd totally forgotten about my friends. "How are they? Where are they?" Marco reached across the seat and took my free hand in his.

"They're okay. Martina is shaken up so Leroy is with her now at her house, but they'll be fine."

"Thank God." A small amount of relief penetrated my sheer panic, and I sucked in a jagged breath. "Have you already called the police?"

Sal's gaze flicked to Marco's in the rearview mirror. "We won't be calling the police," Marco said softly, as if he

ELISABETH GRACE

were trying to explain something to a child.

I spun my head in his direction. "Why the hell not?"

He rubbed at the back of his neck. "The police can't help with this. They have to play by the rules. They have procedures they have to follow. The men who have Daniel do not. We need to have the ability to be as ruthless as they are." The way he said his last statement—with a cold, sinister tone—should have scared me, but it didn't.

"Are you sure that's the right thing to do?" I was so out of my element here.

He looked me straight in the eyes and held my stare. "Trust me. You have my word that we'll get him back."

I pressed my lips together and nodded slowly. "Okay," I whispered before breaking out in sobs against his chest. I'd give myself until we returned to the suite to fall to pieces before I had to pull myself back together.

We went straight up to the suite when we arrived at the Bellagio. The moment the door shut behind us, I began rapid-firing questions at the two men.

"So what's the plan? Do you know where they might be holding him?"

"Calm down," Marco said in his most cajoling voice. He pressed down on my shoulders, forcing me to sit down on the couch behind me.

"I will not calm down! Someone has *kidnapped* my son. Kidnapped! Can you imagine how scared he is right now?"

"We have to play this right. And at the moment, that means waiting. We *will* get Daniel back." I prayed that was a promise. Fuck that. I prayed it was prophecy.

"They're going to call with their demands. They didn't

270

take Daniel because they want to hurt him," Sal said from where he stood on the other side of the living room.

Right. Of course that had to be true. Daniel couldn't do anything for them other than be used as a pawn. Hurting him would accomplish nothing.

"What is it that they're going to want?" I looked from one man to the next, but neither said a word. "Marco, answer me. What do they want?"

Marco abruptly broke eye contact with me, spun around, and stalked toward the exit of the suite. "I have to make some phone calls. I'll be back."

I started to push up off the couch, but Sal raised a hand, indicating for me to stay where I was. "Let him do what he needs to do."

I drew in a deep breath and nodded. Marco would take care of things. Since he'd entered my life, he'd taken care of everything. I could trust him. He'd return Daniel to me.

"I thought they'd only threatened me, Sal."

Sal's fists clenched at his sides. "They did."

"If that's the case, why would they have brought Daniel into this?"

He paused a moment, then said, "I think they probably trailed the van from the hotel and assumed you were in it. The windows are blacked out so you can't see inside. The fender bender was a ruse to get the driver out of the van so they could gain control of the vehicle."

I narrowed my eyes. "But Leroy is a big guy. How could they overpower him?"

"That's just it. The last thing he remembers is bending over to check out the damage to the back of the van. They probably had a hypodermic needle filled with something and knocked him out. Then did the same to Martina."

Poor Leroy. I knew him well enough to know that he'd be beating himself up about this. It was probably killing him that he hadn't been able to protect Daniel.

"He's really okay, though?"

"He is."

I nodded. "So then what?"

"Then they probably went to the back of the van and opened the doors, surprised to find you weren't there. If they'd been watching you, then they'd know you were always with Daniel during the day. Since you weren't there, they took the next best thing. They ditched the van in an empty parking lot rather than leaving it on the side of the road so that it wouldn't draw any attention."

"They knew Marco wouldn't want to call the cops," I finished for him. Sal nodded his affirmation. "How? How could they know that?"

Sal's lips tightened in the corners, but he didn't respond.

The door to the suite slammed shut, and I immediately turned in that direction. Marco stalked in, his once perfectly coiffed hair a little disheveled, the top button of his shirt undone, and his sleeves rolled up.

On anyone else it would have given off the aura of relaxed business casual. On Marco, it was unsettling. He was always so put-together. Marco had had full control of every situation since the moment I'd met him. If he was unraveling, did that mean he'd lost control of *this* situation?

"How'd it go?" Sal's question pulled me from the depths of my own mind.

"It went." With those two words, I knew that he didn't accomplish whatever it was that he'd set out to.

Marco's phone rang from where it was gripped in his

hand. It was as if every other sound in the world had been silenced. Gone was the ticking of the nearby clock, gone was the sound of the cold air whooshing through the hidden vents in the room, and gone was the sound of our breaths. The only sound I could concentrate on was the shrill ring that seemed to slice the silence in half, leaving a gaping chasm in its place—one no words would be able to fill. Because we all knew that this was the phone call we'd been waiting for.

Marco brought the phone to his ear. "Hello."

He listened intently for a minute before responding in Italian.

Listened again.

Replied in Italian.

Listened.

Then hung up.

"What did they say?" Sal asked, which was good because I wasn't able to form any words.

The hand that held Marco's phone dropped to his side. The gesture looked like defeat to me—but no, that couldn't be it. Marco wouldn't give up so easily. He promised I'd get Daniel back. He promised.

"They want the same thing they've always wanted. The one thing I can't give them."

My eyes widened for a moment before I registered that he was walking away. Again.

"Where are you going?" I screamed after him.

"I'll be back," he snapped without turning to look at me and then he left the suite.

I pushed up off the couch and stood. "Why can't he give them what they want?" I stared at Sal, doing my best to intimidate him into telling me, but he was unfazed.

"It's not my place to say."

"Bullshit! I want to know why. What is worth my son's life? Tell me!" Desperate, I gripped the front of Sal's shirt in my hands. "Tell me. I need to know!"

Sal ran a hand through his hair. "I can't. I'm sorry."

No one would tell me what was going on. Who were they protecting? Me, or themselves?

Panic seized me like a vice, and the stronger and tighter it squeezed, the harder it became to breathe. My eyes widened and I clawed at my throat, desperate for air. My lungs burned and I fell back onto the couch behind me as the edge of my vision grew dark.

Sal was saying something, but I wasn't able to make out the words. It sounded as if I were underwater, the words muffled and unintelligible. Something pressed against the back of my shoulders, forcing my head down between my legs.

A small amount of relief came when I was able to siphon in a trickle of air.

And then more.

And some more.

"Are you okay?"

I was able to hear Sal now, and the concern in his voice was clear.

I nodded as best I was able.

"I think you were having a panic attack."

I concentrated on slowing my breathing until it wasn't such an effort anymore, and then I sat up. Sal continued to rub my back.

"You okay?"

"No," I whispered as tears burned in my eyes.

I couldn't do this right now, I reminded myself. I needed to be strong for my son and use my energy to help bring him home. It wasn't the time to fall apart. I could do that once he was safe in my arms again.

Sal dragged me into a hug, and that's when I almost lost it. I must have looked really pitiful if he was showing me affection. I think I'd only seen him crack a smile once, and here he was trying to console me.

"Shh, shh. Marco will be back soon. He can explain everything."

A few minutes later the door to the suite slammed shut. I didn't bother looking up to confirm that it was Marco. I'd grown so accustomed to the man that I didn't need to—his energy, the cadence of his footsteps, the scent of his cologne. All indicated that he was the one who took over embracing me when Sal pulled away.

"Che e' successo?" Marco asked.

"She's demanding to know why you can't give them what they want."

Marco exhaled audibly and pushed me away from his chest so he could look at me.

"Tesoro, you have to trust that I am doing everything in my power to—"

The shrill ring of my cell phone cut Marco off. My gaze darted from Marco to Sal and back again before I sprung up off the couch to dig through my purse on a nearby table.

The phone rang again as I shoved aside my wallet until the lit screen came into view. I tore it from my purse to see who it was.

"I don't know the number," I said, answering the call anyway then putting it on speaker.

"Hello?" I said. Marco stalked over to stand beside me.

"Mom? Mom!" Daniel's voice was frantic. It was such

a shock to my system that I almost dropped my phone.

"Daniel!" I screamed. "Daniel!" Sweat broke out over my entire body and nausea had me clutching my stomach with my free hand.

"Daniel can't come to the phone right now," a sinister voice said. Not Vito, though. There was no accent.

"You bastard! If you do anything to hurt him, I'll—"

A cold laugh sounded through the receiver. "You'll what? Newsflash. You're not calling the shots here, whore."

Marco reached out and took the phone from me. "Leave her out of it," he growled.

"Ah, Mr. Valenti. How nice of you to join the party. We weren't sure that you were taking our threats seriously, so we thought we'd see what your girlfriend thinks of all this."

"You son of a bitch. When I find you, I'm going to take great pleasure in feeding your insides to a pack of rabid dogs." I tugged on Marco's arm, wanting the phone back from him.

Again that laugh sounded through my phone, and it was so void of emotion that every last hair on my arms stood on end. "Have you given any more thought as to what we'd like?"

"You already know my answer. I need more time."

"Time? What for? We've given you more than enough time. We warned you. We told you it would come to this."

"Bastardo! I told you I can't right now. Give me a few days," Marco roared.

A few fucking days? Daniel couldn't stay with those monsters for days!

"Pack your bags and go back to Italy, Mr. Valenti. Do that today, and we'll be sure that Daniel is there to meet you at the airport when you arrive. Don't do it and you'll be heading to the morgue to identify the kid's body."

I whimpered and clutched at myself with shaking hands.

"I need a few more days," Marco said between gritted teeth.

"What will it be, Mr. Valenti?"

I looked to Marco with tears falling from my eyes. He seemed to be fighting an internal battle. "Marco, please," I begged.

"One..." the voice on the phone said.

I gripped Marco's muscled arm and tried to shake him back and forth. "Give them what they want!"

"Two..."

"Please," I begged some more. "I can't lose my son! Don't do this to me!"

"Three. What will it be, Mr. Valenti?"

"Just do what they want!" I screamed. "Whatever it is!"

Marco drew in a breath and closed his eyes for a brief second. "Daniel non avere paure. Andra' tutto bene. Te lo prometto."

"Enough! Last chance, asshole..."

"I can't give you what you want," Marco said.

"Wrong answer."

Daniel's scream echoed out of the phone.

A gunshot rang out.

My son's wail cut off, filling the suite with a deathly silence.

The line went dead.

"Noooooo!" I screamed, the sound of the gunshot reverberating through my head and ripping my soul to shreds.

Marco's face registered the shock I felt through every

cell in my body.

With no warning, vomit raced up my windpipe and I emptied the contents of my stomach all over the carpet. I crumpled to the floor as the reality that I'd lost everything dragged me down into an abyss.

I'd never see Daniel's smiling face again. Never get to rustle his hair or call him buddy. Never get to lay with him in the middle of the night. Never hold him in my arms.

There was no bringing back my son. My world.

The lies and half-truths splintered my fragile heart into jagged pieces of glass that ripped me apart from the inside out. The eyes of the man I thought loved me bore down from above, and the realization hit that he was the one responsible.

He did this.

My heart was a kiln that hardened my despair and transformed it into a rage so monstrous it couldn't be contained. I've been forged in fire and born anew.

He would pay.

They all would.

I'd burn this whole cesspool of a city to the ground until I'd exacted revenge on all of them.

Every. Single. Fucking. One.

USA Today Bestselling Author, Elisabeth Grace has a soft spot for happily ever afters and a hot spot for alpha males. If she's not curled up somewhere with a romance novel in one hand and chocolate in the other you can probably find her typing madly on her keyboard creating her next story. She currently lives outside Toronto, Canada with her husband, two small children, and killer cat.

Let's Connect!
I love to hear from readers! Feel free to connect with me via e-mail at elisabeth@elisabeth-grace.com or via anyone of these social media platforms. I love talking books – even if they aren't my own!
Website: Elisabeth-Grace.com
Facebook Profile: facebook.com/Elisabeth.Grace.790
Gabbing With Grace FB Group:
http://on.fb.me/Hm9mjV
Twitter: @1elisabethgrace
Instagram: authorelisabethgrace

Want to know when my next book is coming out? Besides staying in the loop on new releases I offer my subscribers free content, exclusive giveaways, and a behind the scenes look at what I'm working on next. You can sign up for my newsletter on my website. I take your privacy seriously. I will not sell your e-mail address.

OTHER BOOKS BY ELISABETH GRACE

The Limelight Series - New Adult Romance

Rumor Has It (Limelight #1)

Picture Perfect (Limelight #2)

Collateral Damage (Limelight #3)

The Maine Attraction Series – Erotic Romance

Indecision (Maine Attraction #1)

Indiscretion (Maine Attraction #2)

Standalones – Small Town Romance

Built To Last

Off-Limits Love

ACKNOWLEDGEMENTS

Damn. How about that ending, eh? LOL All right. all right. Put your daggers down I'm just messing with you. ;) Let's get down to business…

When Brandi/Emily's character first popped in my head I was equal parts thrilled and trepidacious. Hmm…a hooker. I want to write a book about a hooker. And not one of those 'finds love on her first trick and never sleeps with another guy' kind-of hookers. An honest to goodness working girl. I knew Brandi was so much more than just *that* in my heart and my challenge was to write her in a way that readers would be able to see that as well. Was it possible to write about an inherently good person doing bad things and have readers root for her? Only you can be the judge of whether I was successful in that endeavour or not. There's a message I was trying to get across with this book. Am I going to come out and tell you explicitly what it was? Nope. I like that each book someone reads speaks to a person on their own level and that each reader pulls their own meaning from it.

Thanks to all the early readers of HOOK. Your support, enthusiasm, and lust for all things Marco make hitting publish on this one a little easier. As I write this I have NO idea how this book will be received and whether anyone besides my family will buy it. LOL Early on when I was writing it I questioned if it would be career suicide to release this one.

This book has a very different tone and subject matter than most of my other work, but I believe in following the muse wherever she takes you and since I'd wanted to write this one for more than a year I decided to take a chance with it. Will everyone cast stones my way for writing about a prostitute and for what happens at the end of HOOK? I don't know the answer to that, but all of your excitement for this book has made me believe that maybe things will be okay even if they do.

A giant hug and thank you to my betas Stacia Newbill, Vicki Shanahan, Meredith Patton, and Roxana Madar who read a really shitty first draft of this book and gave me their thoughts. I appreciate you trudging through the many grammar errors and dangling prepositions to get to the heart of this story. Whether I took your suggestions or didn't, I appreciate the effort you put in immensely.

Which leads me to my editor extraordinaire, Sheri Thomas. I actually managed to get a few smiley faces from you in the comments for this one! LOL You're a picky bitch, but you're *my* picky bitch and this book would not be what it is without all of your efforts. You always treat my manuscripts like your own and have an attention to detail that cannot be surpassed. In fact, I know that you've silently edited this entire Acknowledgements section if you're reading it now. Stop. Just enjoy the thank you! ;)

To my PA and proof reader Shawna Gavas from Behind The Writer...thank you for your friendship, for caring as much as I do about this book, and for being an all around awesome friend!

Linda Russell from SSF went above and beyond for this book! Having you in my corner to set out a game plan of how to roll this book out in the world, as well as remind me over and over and over again of exactly what we decided made life a little easier. Thank God you take notes! ;)

Lisa from The Rock Stars of Romance spearheaded many of the marketing efforts for HOOK. A massive hug to her for putting up with my many messages, questions, and changes as we went along. Having you in my corner made me feel like this book stood a shot in this tough landscape that is indie publishing right now. Thanks so much for all your hard work!

A special thanks goes to Hilaria Alexander for her help with all of the Italian translations. Without your assistance Marco would have some jacked up Google translate version of Italian that just wouldn't do him justice. I'm forever in your debt! Without you Marco wouldn't be the man he is. ;)

This book was written almost entirely between the hours of 4:30 – 6:00 am. Props go to Lucia Franco who was my drag-your-ass-out-of-bed-at-this-god-forsaken-hour buddy. Don't worry everyone...I'm doing the same to get you BURN in a timely fashion. LOL

Lastly, and in no way least to all the readers and bloggers...thank you SO much for your support!!! The book world is a tough, tough, place to be these days and being a reader myself I know how many fabulous books there are that you could give your time and attention to. If you've read HOOK, posted a review, told a friend about it, or messaged me to proclaim your undying love for Hurricane Marco please know that from the bottom of my heart I am grateful to you.

BURN is coming and rest assured you will get all your answers! Until then...